QUICK STORIES & POEMS

VOL. 2

JOSÉ F. NODAR, PUBLISHER

NORTHPORT BOOKSELLERS SPRING FARM NSW AUSTRALIA 2570

Dedication

To our family, our friends, the individual authors in this book we appreciate your support.

Forward

This collection of short stories and poetry is the work of amazing authors who have taken the time to write a story or a poem to bring the reader into their lives.

The idea for this book was simple.

Let authors write and readers read.

I hope you enjoy the variety of stories/poetry in this book.

We thank you for your purchase and support.

Acknowledgements

As the publisher of this book, I would like to acknowledge all those authors, friends, and acquaintances that have had important roles in my life, which inspired me to throughout my life.

To the individual authors who have trusted me with their work and allowed for this book to be created.

Thank you for your trust.

To my wife, my life is everything with you.

Notes

Each author has certified:

1. He/she is eighteen years of age.

2. He/she has taken responsibility for all information in their stories/poetry.

3. Author is aware that this Publisher will not alter the wording of the story to make any correction. Any errors are the responsibility of the author.

4. The author may have received compensation for the use of their story/poetry.

5. To our readers, be mindful that the authors write using British, American, or Australian English, hence some words might look different.

Contents

MERRY CHRISTMAS

I remember staring wide-eyed out of the window at the apocalyptic weather, the icy hailstones being hurled against the glass and bouncing off onto the road, just so I didn't have to look at you. For your part, you were totally focused on driving. Perhaps that was because of the dangerous conditions and your lack of familiarity with the area... Or perhaps you were avoiding me too, as much as we could avoid each other when stuck on the uncomfortably silent car, listening to the hail because we'd given up on listening to each other.

It was late, getting dark, but you pushed on through the night. I restlessly turned as far away from the windscreen as my seatbelt allowed, watching the hard shoulder whizz by. The now-familiar surroundings of my hometown were more comforting than the weather, which reminded me painfully of the storm raging on between us.

Watching the road, I began to tell we were getting close to home now, and the cold, frightened child in me couldn't wait to feel my mother's arms around me and just be home again. The malicious part of me wanted to be home just to spite you, too. The endless back and forth hadn't helped me work out why you didn't want to see my family, even with Christmas just around the corner. But it set me against you. I'm open-minded, but now I could no more compromise with you than I could breathe underwater.

You turned to look at me as you swung the car around the final bend and my beloved childhood home came into view.

"I hope you know I'm only doing this because I love you."

You growled at me, your words as bittersweet as my victory in our argument. You probably don't remember those words as a tragic surrender but as your last stand. But then we never seemed to share a point of view.

And I never did have the sense to leave a finished argument finished, clearly. I hit back, unable to resist.

"Yeah, you love me so much you want me to spend Christmas cooped up alone with you in a crumbly, half-furnished house!"

I'm embarrassed now, as I recall shouting at you in anger, then listening to the long silence, only broken by the hail bouncing off the outside of the car like my words seemed to bounce back at us from every wall inside. Even then, I must have been a little embarrassed, because I opened my mouth to take them back, if only just to stop them echoing around us.

But you had already turned to face me, your focus on the road broken by my focus on us.

"I just wanted us to have one Christmas to ourselves. It's our first after moving in together, remember?"

You seemed tender with me, almost romantic, even after my outburst.

"And the house wouldn't be so bad, it's coming along nicely. Maybe it's just my company you would have a problem with, then."

I rolled my eyes, and my vision blurred for a few moments. Probably just a split second, but it was long enough. Your eyes were still on me, and I wasn't concentrating, so there was no warning from the road ahead, just a sudden jolt and a loud bang! The whole car shook. Looking up, the last thing I remember seeing was the back end of the van we'd smashed into, then total blackness.

When I surfaced from the dark sea of unconsciousness and guilt-ridden dreams, I was laying in the back of an ambulance, a paramedic watching over me, but no sign of you anywhere. I called your name, trying to sit up, but there was nothing but advice to settle back down again and relax until I'd been checked out at the hospital.

But I couldn't and wouldn't relax. I felt sick to my stomach with every lurch of the ambulance, sure my nightmares were all coming true. The rest of that horrible, fateful night is just a blur. The tests, having my broken arm reset, then having to talk to the police, the other driver's tortured expression as he apologised to me, over and over again. Insurance details mix with family reunions but the only memory that stands out is how we never got to spend Christmas together, just me and you.

So that's why I'm sitting here, in the cold, lonely graveyard. Because you always wanted us to have a Merry Christmas together.

Ellie Jay © 2024

DIARY ENTRY

I would find myself drained the moment that I lost you. For years, I have lived with the knowledge it would happen if you left, leaving me with the bitter pill that my life was tied to your breath.

This morning as you left, with my feelings in your hand, you clap to our farewell. Yet I still dutifully bode you well. The sun rose high and as you disappeared from my view, you left me with the ghostly words, 'who knew?'

Oh, I knew.

Years of tiredness and sadness have somehow left me weak. The only things that move in me are the strings that you stapled to my hands and feet. You play those strings with your non-conformist fingers, maverick in their sound and nature—you play my life like a fiddle. Your fingers close together, yet somehow non-whimsical.

With bitter reflection as I write this line, it dawns on me that I may be akin to a puppet. A puppet trapped in a loveless time. You could pick me up and drop me down, I lay where you chose, and I stay where I am to be found.

Oh, I weep at the life I left behind.

Before you, the world said I was flippant and sporadic.

Arbitrary and accidental.

Irregular and undetermined.

I sought the joy of your embrace, and the release from their gaze. I now fear the day you cut these strings and I fall without restraint. Severed threads would dangle from my limp body. Childless cries, and would-be lives, dreams I would never embody.

So, I need you. Oh, how it hurts for me to say so.

My life in your hands, I will dance to any tune that you whistle. You may pull my strings if you see the need to or leave me like a dog that is free to rescue. For I am nothing without the knots that we have tied. Nothing without the heart that beats inside.

Exhausted now, I dance upon this tabletop. As the music plays, I am unable to simply drop.

You will not let me stop.

Your hands act in sync like a Mexican wave, and with them you will one day guide me to my grave. A life of servitude lived for the honour of your name. On my tombstone, it will read:

'A woman unable to cut the strings that bound her, and in this hole, now unbound, is where you find her.

Sam Prosser © 2024

EATING AT WORK IS NO PICNIC

Office work can be very grueling. I must fetch water from the creek (deep sink in the janitor's closet) to make coffee each morning. Then I journey to yonder hunting grounds to trap and bludgeon a fried egg, cheese, and sausage on a toasted bagel. In my little cubicle, I read and answered all the emails from my friends until it is time for a coffee break. I make the rounds to all my fellow co-workers to complain about how overworked and underpaid I am, which usually keeps me busy until lunchtime.

Often, I'm so exhausted from my trips to the cafeteria for breakfast and mid-morning snacks that I no longer have enough energy to make the trek at noon. Fortunately, I am in charge of procurement. Thus, it is no coincidence that I have the only combination personal computer, and a Hot-Dogger machine made by IBM/Ronco. While performing complex calculations with this baby, it is also roasting my weenie and toasting my buns!

An intern asked me for advice the other day. "What does it take to become an executive in this organization?" I told him, "We are looking for people with huge bladders who like to attend meetings all day." I'm always happy to help the little people whenever I can. I say 'little people' not because they are vertically challenged or anything. I am referring to their chances of being promoted around here.

On a mid-morning run for donuts,…not really a run…more like a stagger with a slight limp; I stop at the snack bar to order a tuna fish sub. I always get the foot-long so I can eat half of it immediately. Then, thirty minutes later, I can eat the other half when I get hungry again. The cafeteria lady plopped balls of tuna fish on my sub, which was sufficient for three sandwiches, though I wasn't complaining.

That reminded me of when I moved into a new apartment some years ago. I had gone to the store to stock up on groceries. Taking advantage of a sale, I piled two dozen cans of tuna on the counter.

When the cashier saw that, she asked, "You always eat that much tuna?"

"Why yes. I've been eating a can of tuna almost every day as far back as I can remember."

"Have you ever experienced any side effects from all that fish?"

"Not really…well…there is one thing."

"What's that?" The young gal curiously asked."

"Each spring, I do get a tremendous urge to swim upstream and spawn."

Sometimes, I have had to throw my bloated form in front of the food cart to get it to stop outside my office. Other times, as a matter of life and death to fend off starvation, I've had no choice but to sneak into the employee's lounge to forge for foodstuffs. You can challenge me on this, but I believe I do not need permission to consume anything in the frig that is green and fuzzy…that was not that way originally.

When people eat at their desks, they are considered dedicated or too cheap to go out for lunch. When I take lunch at my desk, some inconsiderate jerk comes barging in, demanding something. I have a name for people like that…I call them 'my boss.' The rest don't have any excuse. I would not be at my desk if I did not want to be disturbed, right? You would think when they see me holding my foot-long in one hand and a Coke in the other, with a whole bag of potato chips in my mouth and a pickle shoved up my nose…that I was having lunch!

They either don't notice or care, but then I suppose it would be too impolite if I continued to choke down my hoagie in front of them. Even though it is noon, the appointed time for lunch according to

International Law, I must shove my food to one side and sit there feigning interest in what they are saying.

While they drone on and on, all I can think about is how my cold food is getting hotter, and my hot food is getting colder. When I return to my little picnic on my desk, it is about as appealing as '…Having a second honeymoon with my wife on our 25th wedding anniversary.' Whatever was firm has gone limp; that which was plump and juicy is now shriveled and wrinkled, and nothing is as fresh and tender as I once remembered. Even the 'mayo' has turned virulent in the heat, and with just one bite, I'll be dead before I hit the floor.

In times like these, I must repair to my supply cabinet and break out the Tostem Pop-Tarts®. I learned how to eat them raw when I was in Japan. Then, I spend the afternoon in a sugar-induced coma. There is much to be said for eating lunch at your desk…like 'DON'T DO IT!"

Following my own advice, I started going to a small cafeteria in our office building, which serves home-style cooking. Every day, there is mashed potatoes, green beans, gravy, and sliced turkey with stuffing, among other things. I just can't seem to stuff myself enough with enough stuffing. If I could, I'd stuff my pillowcase and sleep on it. The cafeteria also has fried chicken, roast beef, and dead fish.

Though you serve yourself, it is not my favorite, 'All you can eat.' It is more like 'All you can afford.'

The first time I was there, I loaded up my plate and took it up to the cashier. A sign prominently read: 'Customers will be charged according to their weight.' When I saw that, I became faint and started to pass out right there in line. The manager rushed over just in time to keep me from falling backward into the cream of broccoli soup, which would not have been good for me…it would not have been good for anyone. He explained the sign meant the weight of my plate, not my weight." Whew! What a relief! I didn't have that much money in my 401k. I doubt even the bank next door kept that kind of cash.

When the little cashier girl weighed my plate, she went to faint. "I've never seen anyone pay this much for lunch before." She asked, "Will that be cash, charge, or do you just want an estimate?" It was a hearty meal, though nothing more than I consume daily, all day. I became very fond of getting a whole breast of turkey, a pound of mashed potatoes with a half stick of butter, a heaping helping of stuffing, globs of green beans, a mess of cranberries, two dinner rolls, and then pouring a bucket of giblet gravy over the whole thing. I would curl up in the corner booth, dig in, and not come up for air until the very last bite was gone.

After washing it down with a Diet Coke, I waddle back to the office, where I spend the rest of the afternoon slumped over my keyboard in a semi-conscious state, in shock from all the cascading carbohydrates in my digestion, causing my levels of insulin coursing through my veins to go into overdrive to ward off the huge assault upon my kidneys, pancreas, liver and whatever else is connected down there.

Right in the middle of my peaceful unconsciousness—someone comes barging in…demanding I do something for them. Some days, it is impossible to get any rest at all. That is when I take refuge in the broom closet to get a few winks.

It has been said that 'breakfast' is the most important meal of the day, though I think you already know I do not like to discriminate. The trouble is, most days, I barely make it to work on time. I suppose I could requisition a hot plate in my cubical to scramble eggs and fry some bacon the way I would at home. However, I would have to review the 'office policy' on sitting in my cubical, wearing nothing but my underwear, and reading the newspaper.

M. David Lutz © 2024

THE SQUIRELL AND THE LADY

There comes a point in life when reality must be faced. That morning, this morning, any morning. When didn't matter, but it still had to happen. Why? Why is it that every early morning you crawl out onto that particular limb and stare for hours at the crawling creature who gnaws on your chosen trees leaves? Wager to say that for the past few weeks its been a relentless repetition in actions that make no sense on the natural level. Animals simply do not fall in love with insects. Or do they? Perhaps, in retrospect, I write you now to explain that very theory to you in full detail. Let's see if my perception impedes upon your reality enough to call it like it really is?

Yes, indeed, you are infatuated by the very bright red six-legged beast that lurks on the branch you sit on. Why else would you go there first, of all places? Surely you know that gathering time has approached, and if you don't keep on task, you'll starve this winter. And this is no jest, and yet you continue to simply stare endlessly as this shiny creature with black spots captures your gaze once again.

The look in your eyes is like stars crashing down to the earth into a black abyss. Nothing and everything exists within the darkness of your pupil, and all this I've gathered only from watching your antics for so long. It's unnatural and yet here I am, a witness to its development. Quite a cute experience nonetheless, but I still wonder how you can love something you've no way to connect with other than to stare at? Or perhaps lift between your human-like hands, that possess such unique dexterity in the animal kingdom that maybe, just maybe, they could be used to caress the object you so desire. I can't yet know this, but what I do know is somehow I've become the unknowing witness to an oddity within nature: the existence of love between two separate species that simply ought not be.

Friend, you're in love with a bug. Not that I have an issue with this, certainly in this day and age we should accept that anyone, thing, or creature ought to be able to love whatever they wish. In your situation, however, I just hope your infatuation doesn't drive you to the point of an accidental squish. I leave you this note now in hopes you'll gain your courage. For I am sure that today, like every other day, will be yet another day spent staring idly at the thing you yearn for most: the ladybug on the limb.

Your Friend,

The Human in the Window

The note was left settled right beside the squirrel's nest, and when it arose the next morning, the squirrel squeaked and tore at the paper. As its nimble fingers ripped the envelope open, beady eyes settled upon the letter, and with every word read, the squirrel began to act more anxious. It fidgeted and waved its tail, curling it in and out every few seconds, only to lash it out in a whiplike motion once again.

Finally, whatever words had to be inked across the page were absorbed, and as the squirrel digested them it bounced down the limb, skittering down the trunk of the tree it lived in and hopping across the backyard towards the tree the ladybug lived on. It was a bit smaller than the other tree, but the squirrel made it up to that spot in a flash. Brown fur fluttered by so quickly that it was almost impossible to tell where the tree began, and the animal ended. The squirrel slowed to a crawl and inched slowly along the branch. Sure enough, there the ladybug was once again: bright, shiny, and beautifully bright red. Just as the squirrel remembered it. The squirrel dipped its nose down to the branch and nudged the tiny bug gently, eyes fluttering to a close as it caressed the little creature.

The sound of a low purr emitted from the squirrel's chest, and as its eyes parted to view the bright red bug again the squirrel found the ladybug had crawled up onto its nose and stayed. Happy and content as ever the Squirrel skittered back down the branch and the trunk of the tree carrying the ladybug on its nose all the way back to its own tree! Amazingly enough, the ladybug never moved a single inch from its perch upon the squirrel's nose, and with the object of its desire in tow the squirrel made way up his tree, across his branch, and dove deep into his nest within the wood.

And that was the tale of the ladybug and the squirrel.

Sai Marie Johnson © 2017

TREVOR'S STORY

Entering the room, Trevor looked around to assess his situation. He had come here voluntarily to give his side of the story and should be able to feel safe. However, his life had taken such a weird direction recently that he had learned to hone his awareness skills and evaluate all new surroundings with regards to security and safety.

The journalist came in behind him, she was known to his circle of friends, as small as that circle was, to be fair, honest, and open-minded. His story was sure to test those qualities, he shook her hand, and she gestured to an armchair indicating that he should sit.

She sat in the chair opposite him, and her assistant clipped a microphone to his collar, while she adjusted her own. She prepared her notepad, looked at Trevor and smiled, then took out a pen and pencil and placed it on her lap.

"We need to get the levels right for the audio, so let's use this opportunity to introduce ourselves," touching her chest she smiled again and said, "My name is Carol Tate, I am a freelance journalist currently researching a spike in the reporting of paranormal events. In regard to that I would like to interview you and hear what you can contribute to my study."

Trevor smiled back, "Please just call me Trevor, we can discuss how that name came to be in due course, and subject to the terms and conditions already discussed, I will be delighted to talk to you."

Carol looked over to the young man sitting at the audio mixer and recorder and received a thumbs up.

"I guess we're good to go Trevor, shall we get started?"

"Why not?"

Trevor shuffled a little in his seat to get comfortable and placed his hands in his lap. He looked at Carol and smiled, then said, "Where do you want to start?"

"Normally I like to start at the beginning, but from the limited understanding that I have of your previous work and what it has allowed you to do, I understand that may not be appropriate. So, you choose."

"Fair enough, I won't be able to go into things that are still protected under the Secrets Acts, but I can give you an overall idea of what started this whole thing. Now, I am going to say something that will seem implausible to you, this all started when I was a lot older."

Carol's head shot up from gazing at her notepad and she had a confused look on her face.

"I know, I know, but bear with me here. As a somewhat older man named Dr. Peter Castell, I was involved in a highly sensitive research program that was investigating the plausibility of time travel."

"And did you succeed?" Carol asked.

"Yes and no Miss Tate. Yes and no. Much of what I will tell you this afternoon will require you to first suspend your disbelief and secondly attempt to understand the true nature of paradox."

Carol scribbled a few notes then said, "I'll give it a go Trevor, but how, just how in hell did you used to be an older man?"

"Let's try and explain that then. A little later I am going to tell you that time travel is non-existent, but also that, by most people's understanding of the concept, we actually achieved it."

"At the point in the story that these events took place we knew even less about the true nature of existence, and we had no real idea what consequences could occur as a result of our attempts at the manipulation of space and time."

Tapping his chest, he continued, "Peter Castell had a troubled youth. After a successful stint in the military, he, I mean I, was wounded in a counter-terrorist operation to the extent that my career was effectively over. It was the only thing I had ever been really good at, and I really was good at it."

"When I left the military I had a nice little sum of money for those days, and I pissed it all up against the wall. I began to spiral into a lifestyle that was leading me to an early grave. It all looked like it was going to end with a suicide attempt in a central London Park."

"As part of my research into the project I effectively went back in time to monitor my behaviour and witnessed my own attempted suicide. While trying to stop it I triggered something that we later learned to call 'The Significance Algorithm' and knocked my younger self into a kind of limbo, a holding environment so to speak, which allowed existence to sort out any anomalies."

"A series of events, which we interpreted incorrectly as it turned out, caused me to rescue myself from that holding environment and return both my younger and older selves to what we then thought of as the present."

"Then thought of?" Carol asked.

"We'll get to that Carol, yes there were two of me, separated by over 40 years, living in the same time frame, but we soon learned that such a thing was an abomination to existence and we both became very sick, in fact we both started dying."

"Wait, let me get this straight. Existence itself dictated that you couldn't both be in the same time frame?"

"Again, can we get to that later?" Carol nodded.

"If we didn't want both versions to die one of us had to go voluntarily. My older self took that choice as his body was reacting very badly and breaking down faster than this one. He took his own life leaving me behind but, as Peter Castell was now dead, we had to create a new identity for me, so Trevor was born, or rather created."

"What happened next, well over a period, was that I absorbed everything that my older self-had ever learned and experienced. I became a man in his mid-twenties with the accumulated knowledge and experiences of the same man forty years older."

Carol looked at Trevor, not knowing exactly what to believe. This could all be some fantasy or psychosis, but Trevor had been highly recommended to her as part of her research. She should hear him out at least.

"How did that feel Trevor?"

"Both incredible and frightening, I had memories of things that I physically hadn't experienced yet. I felt both supercharged yet anxious at the same time. Having the project to deal with, and going back to leading it, helped get my mind off of the personal issues and gradually I became more and more comfortable with it."

"And here you are now?"

"Oh, a lot happened between then and now, that was just the start, the preamble if you like."

"So where do we go next?"

"Well, the project continued and grew, I'm afraid I can't go into specifics, but we did some very good humanitarian work, but as with everything there were elements that wanted to use it as a weapon. To be fair we had always expected a tactical aspect to the project but hoped that it would be used wisely and justly."

"More importantly though, our understanding of the nature of existence grew exponentially. While it's fair to say that we still don't know much, we, in fact, know a whole lot more than when we started the project and the research."

"Such as?"

"Now, if you thought that what I told you just now was unbelievable, you're going to have a lot of trouble with these concepts. So, I ask you to bear with me and reserve judgement until later. We arrived at a phrase that encapsulated our understanding of space and time, and that is 'Everything is always already happening'."

"Time really is a construct that those of us trapped in existence use to make sense of things, but in fact, there is no past, no future, just a whole lot of now."

"And.. you lost me," Carol said.

"I'm not surprised, I got lost a lot trying to understand all of this. First of all, try to grasp the idea that everything we know is made of frequencies Waves are everything and everywhere and the infinitely possible combinations and interference patterns of those frequencies create what we think of as reality. Now, before you get too bogged down try and understand that they all exist now, they just exist, not then, not soon, but now. You don't have to travel backwards or forwards in time, you just have to kind of slide into a new set of already existing frequencies and experience that 'now'."

"What we discovered is that everything is made up of primary and secondary datasets of frequencies and that sub-sets of those frequencies identify the concept of when and where something appears to be. By altering those subsets, you can appear to move something in, what we consider to be, space and time. It's all relative to our understanding because in fact everything already is."

"So, Trevor, are you telling me that you actually achieved this, can you summarize what you actually managed to do?"

"Very simply, Carol, we worked out what the desired subset frequencies would be and bombarded a subject with those frequencies and they tripped to the new instance of reality."

Carol held up her hand to stop him talking, "And that's supposed to be putting it simply?"

"Let me try again, and I'm not judging here Carol, this is beyond cutting edge stuff. Have you heard of something called entrainment?"

"I have not, Trevor."

You know how if you're trying to relax, say during a massage or in meditation, they play soothing music set at a very low beats per minute rate?"

"Yes, and I hate pan pipes because of that." Trevor laughed at her quip.

"Well, it doesn't have to be pan pipes, famously Baroque music is usually performed at 60 bpm and listening to it, in a quiet atmosphere, will slow down your heart rate and calm your mind. Similarly, if you are at a hard rock concert your adrenaline will flow and your heart rate will spike accordingly. This is called entrainment. So, we bombarded the subject with the desired data sets of frequencies, entrainment took over and the subject would move to the desired instance, thereby appearing to travel through either space and/or time."

Carol looked up sharply, "Woah, so you're saying that you did this, you moved objects like that?"

"Not just objects, people too."

"Through time?"

"Well, I hate to flog a dead horse here but factually not through time just to an instance that appeared that way."

Carol was doing her best not to appear flustered, "Can you just humour me and my newness at all this and let me think of it as through time?"

"And through space, sure we can do that."

"Great, I might make some headway here now. So how would this cause an increase in paranormal events being reported."

"I can't say for certain that it has Carol, I don't know if there's enough data to say that but there is always that possibility. To let you wrap your mind around this concept a little better I will ask you to imagine something. Try to think of reality as a whole lot of stacked, micro thin slices, of reality and that they are all made of variations of frequency interaction. Now imagine that we change one of those frequencies significantly, and that the ripples spread out and 'nudge' the other instances. Do you see where I'm going here?"

"Are you saying that moving something from one instance to another might cause interference to both?"

"As long as you leave the word 'might' in there I'll go along with that."

Carol scribbled a couple of notes and nodded.

"As I said, I can't go into details, but we moved some huge amounts of stuff and if that is a possible cause we could definitely have made some ripples that may even have allowed instances to overlap, and that 'could' have caused some events to occur that might be considered paranormal. But there's more Carol, quite a lot more."

Carol looked up, "Do you need to take a break?"

"No, if you're good, so am I"

"So, what more is there?"

"There were three of us that made a lot of trips. We called them trips to avoid falling into the past and future language trap. We had several agents that we used to make trips depending on the actual nature of the mission. However, three of us made more than any of the others. We had a male and a female operative, both with military and intelligence backgrounds, which made an enormous number of trips and, of course, myself."

Carol looked up again, "So do you also have a military background, Trevor?"

"As I said earlier, I do, I was a counter terror agent for the Royal Air Force Regiment for a few years until an injury forced my retirement. I made a very large number of trips and over time something happened to me, causing me to become something more than I was at the start of the project."

"Care to explain?"

"Sure, during everybody's life they constantly evolve to different degrees. Consider, we start off learning to walk, we have to watch where we place every footstep, but gradually we don't look down anymore, we learn the skill to see where everything is around us and walk easily. This is a form of personal evolution, an acquisition of new skills common to everyone. Similarly, when we first trip we need the aid of being bombarded with frequencies, but gradually, over time and with experience, we have been able to learn to trip without that. A few of us developed the ability to 'tap into' or recognize the frequencies in which we exist and slowly began to develop the ability to change them and trip unassisted."

"Why didn't this happen to every agent?" Carol asked.

"I think it may have to do with our military training and experience. We have been trained to become acutely aware of our surroundings; to identify hazards and prepare for them and I think this may have boosted our ability to incorporate the frequency information defining our surroundings and with experience learn how to change them."

"Trevor, you're going to need to explain what all that means to me in a language I can understand."

"Would a demonstration be better?"

"If that's possible, sure."

Trevor took a sip from the glass of water and placed it back on the table. "Carol, can you move that glass closer to yourself please?"

She picked up the glass and placed it just a few inches from her notepad, "Okay?"

"That's fine, now watch it closely Carol."

She focussed her attention onto the glass, but it instantly vanished. "What the fuck??" and when she looked over to Trevor she saw that it was in his hand as he took a sip.

He placed the glass back onto the table and asked her, "Is that okay for now?"

"That's creepy is what that is Trevor, how did you do that?"

"I don't really know Carol; the descriptive process is beyond me. Just as I don't know how I change the focus of my sight when I look from near to far, I just know how to move things like that."

"Do all three of you have the same abilities?"

"No, it differed with each of us, all revolving around the same skill set and all using the same techniques but just to different levels."

"I'm staggered Trevor, I don't know what to say."

"So, we're done?"

"No!!! I have more questions, and I need to know if there's any connection between what I just witnessed and the increase in paranormal incidents."

"Well, you just saw one more incident right there, although to be fair, it's paranormal to you but now completely normal to me. It is entirely possible that people have seen either my colleagues, or myself, appear to move things or sometimes seem to disappear or appear. Although we do try to take care not to freak people out."

"Are you now telling me that you can move like that too?

Suddenly she was looking at an empty chair.

"Better that I show you again," his voice came to her from behind and she turned to see him standing there.

"Holy shit, that's not a good way not to freak people out, I'm freaking out big time right now."

"Are you ready for one more freak out?"

"I guess..."

"Do you know everything that was in your bag when you came out this morning?"

"Mostly, yes."

"So, you'd recognize something that was not there when you left your home?"

"Almost certainly."

"Then please check your bag."

Carol took her bag from the back of her chair and opened it cautiously. There, right on top of the other contents was a small keyring with the words 'Project Wave' engraved on the metal disc. She held it up and examined it carefully and asked when he had put it there.

Trevor walked around the desk and sat back down, as Carol followed his movements she felt a small movement at her back.

"Was that.. you.."

Trevor grinned and said "Yeah, sorry about that."

"I am totally confused," Carol said.

"Don't try and understand everything, simply accept that there are things that can happen that you won't be able to understand."

Carol took a drink of water and agreed, "That's probably a good idea."

"Trevor, there were a lot of conditions placed on this interview, secrecy and privacy being one of the primary ones, could you elaborate on why that was?"

"Well, I'm a wanted man, we can cover why later, but the irony is that I keep letting them catch me, but they can never hold me because of what you just saw. Sometimes I even let them cuff me and just trip out when I feel like it."

Carol laughed a little, "I can see why that would be frustrating for the captors."

Looking at the interviewer Trevor made a snap decision to tell her a lot more. "Let me explain something that may be even harder to understand."

"Harder than what we've already covered?"

"Well, that will be up to you. I have become something that has rarely existed and that is completely self-aware. I mean that in the sense that I don't just think that I am a set of frequencies interacting, I know it. I understand it and as such can identify with all other frequencies around me. Watch this please."

Carol watched as Trevor raised his hand, formed his fingers into a point and slid them into the very structure of the table. His hand melted through the hard wooden surface and was, quite simply half inside the table and half out.

"Whoa." Carol's eyes widened and she almost forgot to breathe. "That's an illusion, right?"

"Everything's an illusion Carol, everything. Here's the deal though, I can walk through walls, reach inside a building, and move to anywhere or any 'time' that I want to. I previously held top secret clearances and spearheaded a Government Committee that organized highly classified operations."

Trevor took a deep breath and continued, "As my self-awareness grew, I held back the nature of my abilities from my colleagues, but when I found out that a few other members of my previous team could also do extra ordinary things I confided in a few people."

"Gradually though, some people found out, or suspected various things, and I became perceived as a security threat. The committee that I chaired was disbanded, or I think reformed but without me, and a warrant was issued for my urgent arrest. I went along with it all for a little while, but whenever I got bored, I would trip somewhere else. You can imagine how this infuriated the agencies looking for me I'm sure."

Carol had put down her pen and pad and was just watching Trevor as he spoke. "I can, that must be very frustrating for them." She reached under her desk and pulled out one of the original belts that the Wave members wore to bale out of a trip and return to their base of operations. She placed it on the desk and said, "As part of my research I got hold of one of these from a source, can you tell me what it is?"

Trevor smiled and said, "Of course, but can I borrow a piece of paper from your pad and your pen first please?"

Carol pushed the pad and pen cross the table and Trevor started to write, just a paragraph, then he turned the pad over so that what he had written was obscured.

"That is a bale out belt, we used it to abandon a trip in an emergency situation, it immediately bombarded us with frequencies and zapped us back to the base."

Carol prodded at the belt and asked him, "Is it safe to try on, I'd like to try it on please."

"I'm sure it is, just don't pull any handles."

Carol tried on the belt, and it fit badly and felt chunky. "It's heavier than I thought it would be."

"That's an early model, we eventually got them a lot slimmer and lighter than that, it was based on an old military belt style."

"Can I see how it looks on you?" Carol smiled, took off the belt and pushed it across the table.

"Sure," and Trevor stood and put the belt around his waist. "Feels like an old friend," and he grinned.

Carol reached under the desk and pulled out a small remote, pressing one button a couple of small lights on the belt started to glow and a very gentle hum could be heard. "Trevor I'm sorry about this, but a girl's gotta eat, and they paid me a wad of cash to get you to put that on."

"So, this is bombarding me with the frequencies of this instance to get me to stay here, correct?"

"Fucked if I know Trevor, my interest stopped when you put the fucking thing on."

Trevor laughed, long and loud, a head back comic book villain kind of a laugh. "Well, I gotta be going anyway Carol, or whatever your name is, I left you a note." The belt fell to the floor as Trevor simply vanished.   Carol looked around to the 'sound engineers' and yelled "I'm keeping the money you fucking muppets."

She reached over and picked up the pad and laughed as she read the note.

"You obviously weren't paying attention when I told you just some of the things I can do. I knew exactly how this would play out and exactly what you will say when you read this note .. 'Really' … I knew."

Carol laughed more and simply said, "Really..."

Peter Draper © 2022

CITY POETS

I am envious of poets
who live close to nature
whose words spring from the
loamy earth under their feet and
spray forth to glisten and sparkle
in their light-filled air. Who stand

in moonlight listening for the sound
of owls and sometimes for peace and
the quiet of things. Who know and speak
the names of every familiar plant and bush
and flower and move our hearts with stories
of the passing of time and love and the

inevitable naturalness of death. Here
in my asphalt-encircled capsule
of a house with forty-seven cafes and three
supermarkets within walking distance
there is only the pure blue of the far off
Australian sky. On my way down

the street I pick up empty beer bottles
and toss them in the nearest
recycling bin. Beside the footpath

a eucalypt has died on the
doorstep of an expensive
apartment. Confined to one small

square of earth and weeds, its elegant
trails of white-bloomed leaves are now
shrivelled and brown. People living there
pass it every day but for them nature
is an unknowable foreign country.
Down the street, a man is knocked

off his bike by a car that veered across
the bicycle lane. In the Syrian coffee shop
a trio of well-dressed businessmen meet to
gossip in Russian. A customer tells of how
he lost his job because of covid. He has found
a wallet in the street and is searching
for its owner on Facebook.

In the world of city poets, all hope
for humanity is not lost but lives on
between the cracks in the relentlessly
hard grey surface of our everyday lives.

Maree Gladwin © 2024

PAST POEM TO FUTURE CHILD OF MINE

If you ever see the harsher things,
The crueller things,
The stab right through to the heart of things.
Then remember the nicer things,
The kinder things,

The one plus one makes beautiful things.
If you're ever hurt by the colder things,
Then find some love in the warmer things,
The lasting things,
The one plus one makes new little things.

For I have seen some scary things,
Some lonely things,
The one take two make painful things.
But I never lost sight of the little things,
I never lost touch of the real things,

The truthful things,
The love plus love makes amazing things.
And one day you will be a thing.
Not a dream nor a hope but a tiny thing.
Akin to the lighter things,

The smelly things,

The furniture plus you makes broken things.

Untouched by the frightful things,

The troubling things,

The bills plus bills make no present things.

But you will have me and all my worthful things,

My personal things,

My past and future things,

So please, future child of mine, be delicate when you pull upon my heartstrings.

Sam Prosser © 2022

AMELIA'S COMING FOR LUNCH

Let me tell you, right at the out-set, that I do not know Amelia.

This is how I learned about her.

It is a hot clammy Friday afternoon around 2.30pm. I'm on a train heading home from the city. I have a seat in one of those carriage set aside for wheelchair occupants. At the moment there is only myself, and an Indian lady, and a man in a suit, sitting opposite me. There is a steady stream of traffic as teenage students pass from one carriage to another. They look sweaty, shirts sticking to their backs, and they are loud. Indian lady shrugs her shoulders at me, and we both smile.

We are about to find out what loud really means.

Two stops on, a portable ramp crashes with a whiplash crack at the carriage door. A huge woman in a wheelchair is propelled up it and swerved into the carriage. Including the boy, pushing the wheelchair, there are four children, young adults, ranging in age from about fourteen to eighteen years. The first thing I notice about the woman is her legs. Inflamed, extraordinarily swollen. It hurts to look at them. The woman's feet are spilling over the straps of her sandals. The two boys and the youngest girl are yelling at each other. It's escalating toward flash point. They all have phones in their hands. The eldest girl, legs wrapped round each other, is curved and folded into her phone. The movement of her fingers on the face of the phone is like a ballet, quick, precise, elegant. This girl, without looking up, says "Ma."

Ma booms into the standoff between the three to cut it out or she will take their phones of them. They become quiet immediately. This silence lasts for the next two stops, but a sullen atmosphere prevails.

The eldest boy erupts with venom when another line of school students attempts to use the carriage as a passageway.

"Watch it. There's a woman in a wheelchair. There's not enough room to get past. Show some respect."

The students aren't cowered by him. They slow down a little and carefully inch their way past the wheelchair. The eldest boy glares at them but Ma smiles at the extra care the students take. The train glides into another station and three police men get on. They are big men made much bigger with the paraphernalia bulging around their waistlines. They have guns. The red-haired policeman recognises the man in the suit and moves into the carriage to talk to him. The children, apart from the girl with the ballet fingers, consider this to be a token of friendliness for them as well.

"Is that a real gun?" asks one of them.

"Yes." He grins indulgently. "But you can't touch it"

That grin opens the flood gates, and he is peppered with questions. They are not touching the gun, but they are touching him and other parts of the belt.

"Look at all these things Lucy. Look" One of the children shakes her shoulder.

Lucy looks up from her phone, flicks a glance at the policeman's face, and then at the gun. Her disdain is evident. Turns back to her phone. That glance took two seconds perhaps, but in those two seconds the policeman takes note of liquid amber eyes and is transfixed, oblivious to the fact that the children are pressing closer. The other policemen are alert to this, and the one with the hardest eyes and the thinnest lips moves in.

"Back off kids." He is not threatening but his voice matches his face, and the children peel away immediately.

"I know you" says Ma. "We've met. You worked with my cousin at Wollongong station."

The policeman does remember her. Some chit chat is exchanged. "This your brood. You've got your hands full here." Ma shrugs. She has established her status. He addresses his red-headed colleague. "Next stop ours, mate." The young policeman throws a backward glance at Lucy, but she is oblivious to it.

The eldest boy is aggrieved and upset.

"He didn't remember me. He remembered you Ma. He didn't remember me."

"Why should he?" Ma asks genuinely surprised.

"Because he's the first cop who ever charged me. No heart, the bastard. Even when I told him you were in a wheelchair."

"That was his job." Ma snaps at him. The thin sliver of status has slipped away. "You got what you deserved."

The boy flinches, his face reddens. There are tears in his eyes. I feel for him. He is hurting. He, too, wants status. To be memorable. Lucy looks up and states "Amelia's coming for lunch tomorrow."

There is an explosion of joy. The eldest boy is now jumping up and down. The two youngest are punching their fists in the air. "What are we going to eat?" yells the youngest girl.

"Quieten down" commands Ma. "Let me think or there won't be a lunch."

Lucy's preciseness matches the precision of her ballet fingers. "We'll have chicken schnitzel, chips and mushy peas." They all nod in agreement. Amelia loves the way Lucy makes the schnitzel, and if there a lot of chips they only have to have a small helping of the mushy peas. The desert presents a problem. There is vanilla ice-cream left in the freezer, but the budget won't allow for anything extra this week.

The youngest boy says importantly that if he weeds the garden for the next-door neighbours, he can pick lots of strawberries from their garden patch. He glows in the thumbs up sign all his family give him. The train is slowing down for the next station. There is the clang of the portable ramp, and the family departs. We hear the fading strains of "Amelia's coming for lunch, Amelia's coming for lunch."

One of the passengers joining the carriage is a man wearing the vest of railway employee. He is on the phone, and we hear "Are they closing the station down?" Haven't caught the guy yet?" "How many police." He's off the phone and becomes chatty. There's been a stabbing at Campbelltown station. The Indian lady and I look at each other. We've weathered the washing machine of emotions. We are rolling with the punches.

Home. Showered. Crisp white wine in chilled glass. The television news announces the police have found the stabbed man and are investigating the incident. There is a glimpse of a man on a stretcher as the paramedics wheel him into an ambulance.

And the wish comes into my mind, that, as Amelia sits before her banquet of chicken schnitzel, chips and mushy peas followed by desert of vanilla ice-cream with the bartered strawberries, she brings to that table the kind of strength that will throw a protective mantle around the family. That the young boy, smarting with tears in his eyes, will never lie bloodied on a stretcher, aching with the desire to be of note. Pleading with whoever gets there first, that they will remember him.

Maybe it will become enough that Amelia keeps coming for lunch and that she remembers him.

Maybe. I hope so.

Susannah Thompson © 2024

GRACE IS ON DISPLAY

The Greek word "charis" means unearned, undeserved, and unmerited favor. It is the origin of the word "grace." It is a gratuitous favor that accomplishes nothing. Grace is a present. All men see grace, but not all can experience it. What will you do when you hear the word "grace"? Consider Jesus by Himself! The Lord Jesus Christ is synonymous with the gospel and grace, and humility is their ally. The humble mentality is where the power of grace works. A follower of Jesus Christ needs to approach the throne of grace. Why should you be afraid to approach Jesus Christ when He has already paid the full price for your sins?

The grace of the apostle Paul was marvelously expended. He comprehended the Lord Jesus Christ, and he was aware of his mission. It makes sense why Jesus states, "We do not lose heart since we have this ministry because we have received mercy." You are pressuring the Lord to reveal more to you. This is if you understand what grace is and who the Lord Jesus Christ is. You have to grasp the gospel to be able to feel God's power. The Lord Jesus Christ is the source of grace!

When God is at work in a person's life, He lets His grace do the hard work. He doesn't need that person to do anything special, since His grace is enough. For a Christian, understanding grace is crucial. Understanding grace entails studying the thoughts of the Lord, Jesus Christ. "Put on the Lord Jesus," declares the word of the Lord. You see, without knowing how grace operates, it is impossible to put on the Lord Jesus. What gives a Christian such assurance is God's grace. There is a constant need to exalt Jesus Christ. Imagine the situation if Jesus Christ had not died on the cross.

You may be wondering: Where is truth, and where is grace? There is a connection between truth and grace. Truth exists where grace does, and grace exists where truth does. Let me show you how Jesus Christ brought grace and truth, while Moses gave the law." "But grace and truth came through Jesus Christ," it says once more. Whoa! Have you observed that? It sounds amazing. Grace and truth are the two terms that will be our main topics. Recall that Moses received the law, and who was the channel for the revelation of grace and truth? Jesus Christ, the Lord! You have to mumble the name of Jesus anytime you utter these two words.

One needs to believe the truth to first feel God's grace. Without believing the truth, you are unable to receive God's grace. In reality, believing the truth unlocks the grace of God applied to the cross. The truth is the doorway to grace. Again, I say it: There is a door to grace. What's the real story? When Jesus declared, "I am the way, the truth, and the life," do you recall? I'm hoping you know about it. The response is, "I am." Furthermore, who is "I am"? Jesus Christ, the Lord. On one side, he exudes honesty, and on the other, grace. When Jesus challenged the Pharisees and Scribes, He told them to study the scriptures. The scriptures bear witness to Him. He repeated, "They will know the truth, and it will set them free when they keep studying the scriptures."

Even though it is unpopular, people can access the truth and apply it with grace. God's grace is evident to everyone. But not everybody is feeling it. God's grace is being enjoyed by those who believe in the Lord Jesus Christ. Rejecting the truth is the most harmful thing you can do. And when you do that, you end up where? You turn down grace. My dear readers, you will encounter the truth when you meet Jesus Christ. You will learn everything from the gift that is the Holy Spirit. And it's true that "everything"

Many individuals fear the truth, even though they desire to hear it. Even so, individuals cannot accept the truth when someone shows it to them. They face the threat of a bomb demolishing them. You are whole in Him (Jesus), my dear. It also implies that you can have as much grace and honesty as you desire. You will learn grace and truth from Jesus. Although they expected Him to tell them the truth, the Jews rejected Him due to their blindness. They wanted to hear the truth. You need grace to understand the truth. Once you do, it will help you live well in this sinful world. It's the will of God to give the truth to His children for them to function.

If grace is not drawing us in, we are unable to know the truth. We are not able to draw ourselves to the truth; grace is the one guiding us there. Before you can uncover the truth, you must first find grace. Furthermore, grace opens the door to the truth, as we have been saying. The truth lies concealed within grace. You must come to grace to discover the truth and the treasures of the truth. The Lord Jesus Christ spoke: "You will know the truth, and the truth will set you free." Jesus was only teaching that you can't know the freeing truth until you first believe in Him.

The grace of God has appeared to all men. Now a question: where did grace appear? The answer is so simple: ON THE CROSS! You have to hear the gospel of grace before you come to the truth. Listen here; the truth cannot make you free, but the knowledge of the truth can. What is the knowledge of the truth? Here are some answers. Salvation is only by grace. You have nothing to do to enter heaven. It is only by faith in Jesus. You can't do anything to please the Lord. You must understand that water baptism can't save you. To mention a few, you have paid for your sins. And if you know this is true, it will make you free. You will be free from bondage. When the gospel comes to you, that is a cover; you have to believe the gospel and enjoy the truth in it. You better throw away the veil of legality and realize that there is grace to save. I didn't become a Christian by my power. I am a Christian by grace. I have a Christian grace telling me so. Grace guides my life, and that is why I love it. I am a stranger to this world because grace is on my side. But I see Jesus!

The divine grace is life's force. Life as a Christian is obscure and secretive. Grace protects Christians. Those who haven't converted can't understand them.

Grace makes the scriptures alive.

How much time did God take to write the words of God? What number of generations are there now? You are reading God's words now. Thousands of grandfathers and grandmothers have read them before you. Why? Because the words are alive because of grace! You study the scriptures, dear ones. Not because you want to, but because grace makes it possible.

The papers bore the inspired words of God, intended to help us know and comprehend Him. The Holy Spirit illuminates what God has written.

Both the words and the Lord Jesus Christ are alive today. The tool that helps us comprehend who Jesus Christ is is God's grace. Grace makes the phrases pierce the soul. A Christian understands the words of truth because of grace. A Christian can distinguish between truth and error because of grace. In a Christian life, grace makes the words meaningful. Before men, Grace is unbelievable.

Grace will pique your interest in the words when you open your Bible. Grace will make you want to read the Bible. To memorize, apply, speak, and understand its words. And to teach and preach them.

Grace helps you realize that the Bible is adequate. Grace helps you see that the Bible is enough. Throughout it, one can find revelations. Grace teaches you that the Bible contains all the answers to life's questions. And as you study the Bible, grace will provide you with the solutions.

To you, God's grace is everything. Even if we are at a loss for words, grace inspires us to express the amazing things that God has done. Grace is always there to support us, even in moments when we are unable to speak. Thanks to grace, God's words are alive. We must comprehend and be aware of the workings of God's grace. God is aware that redemption from sin requires grace. Furthermore, you must remain on the grace ground for God to start operating in your life.

The reign of grace.

The grace is captivating. And no matter what, grace is impervious to sin. The Lord Jesus Christ is at the center of and related to everything. It's important to realize that the Lord Jesus is the key figure in the kingdom of grace. His death was not in vain.

When someone believes in the Lord Jesus Christ, grace works in all areas of their life.

A Christian's life is not hard. Odd things might happen to him, but grace is there to help him overcome them.

Never forget that God's grace rules your life. To name a few, there is grace reigning in sin. There is grace reigning in adversity and frailty. Also in disappointment and rejection. Grace also reigns in failure and persecution.

God cursed the Moabite tribe, to which Ruth belonged. Ruth was later identified as belonging to the generation of the Lord Jesus Christ. While tending to the sheep, King David ascended to the throne of Israel. Hannah gave birth to Samuel despite being sterile and unable to bear children. Though his brothers detested him, Joseph went on to become prime minister. Do you know how the kingdom of grace works?

God uses things that the world rejects. They see them as nothing more than bases. They mock, ignore, and find them useless. Are you aware of the reason? to manifest His glory and for His grace to reign in those areas. God looks for empty, weak objects to fill them with His grace.

Have you given your life to the Lord Jesus Christ, dear? I want to remind you that you can fill yourself with grace. You can carry yourself to unexpected places. Instead of concentrating on the past, pay attention to the Lord Jesus Christ. Jesus has covered the entire amount, so you don't need to worry. All you need to do is trust in Christ Jesus the Lord and let God's grace rule over everything in your life.

Legalism is the enemy of grace.

You should read the book of Galatians because it protects grace from legalism, which is its enemy. Individuals attempting to poison the Galatian brethren enraged the apostle, Paul. The legalistic instructors sought to twist the grace. It had saved the Christians in Galatia by faith. Adding something to God's grace nullifies grace. Furthermore, God's grace will not impact you in any way.

Legalism is the work of the flesh [the body], and grace is the work of the Spirit of God. The flesh and the Spirit of God cannot work together; neither agree. Grace hates the works of the flesh. When the flesh is in control, grace stops working. Legalistic practices glorify sinful nature, but grace glorifies the works of Christ. You know that God hates sin and cannot tolerate it. The scriptures state, "God resists the proud but gives grace to the humble." Legalisms produce pride, but grace produces humility. God resists the proud and is merciful to the humble. A proud person is legalistic, and he is the enemy of grace. A proud person is against the cross of Christ because they are not thankful for what Christ has done. He bases his perspective on himself, not on Christ. He thinks that he will go to heaven with his strength and work. This person explains scriptures based on his foolish knowledge. He does not do it according to the Spirit of God.

Damian Nakare II © 2024

MONDAY PICK ME UP

Monday, the day that is the roughest of the week,

Try not to be too weak or you will be done by the end of the week,

The beginning of the week is the hardest of all, but not the craziest of all,

The week will be hard, but then you get to be you when you come home,

To be there and the be home is a crazy thing to be.

But you get to come home to see to community that is to be,

Nothing to see, nothing to hear, but the pain and anguish that you may fear,

Just know that it may be the end of the week, but there truly is nothing to fear.

Curtis L. L. Herbold © 2024

CATASTROPHIC CATASTROPHE OF CATACYLSMIC CATSEQUENCES

Now I am not gonna say that any man who owns a cat is a sissy, not because it isn't true, but because some of those guys could kick my manly butt. Just the same, I've been seeing a tragic but seldom discussed form of mental illness most prevalent with our more senior citizens who hereafter shall simply be referred to as 'really old farts.' From my own experience, I can tell you it is very sad and unpleasant to witness. Someone in your family probably has or will have this illness.

It was a long time ago, but I can remember it as if it had happened…a long time ago. My old man, already in his sixties, took me to visit my grandparents, whom I had not seen since the last time I saw them. It was not that I wouldn't have liked to visit them, especially since I lived in northern Florida, and they lived in Tampa. However, I only ever saw them when my dad took me. I was not accustomed to visiting them on my own. My dad was uncomfortable with the idea of me seeing them by myself. This made me suspect there was some sort of cover-up going on. I'd always had my suspicions about Grandpa.

He was from the old country (Germany) and looked like Hitler. Later, when I was much older and bolder, I finally asked him—very cautiously, what he knew about the Führer. In his broken English, always filled with an abundance of expletives, he explained he was only fourteen when his brothers bought him a ticket to come to America; Hitler had just started his rise to power. I had no choice but to accept his explanation, as I didn't have the phone number for Simon Wiesenthal, but I would continue to keep an eye on him just the same.

My dad and I were there to fix and clean up Gramp's place before the Health Department carted the old folks off to wherever they cart old folks. Even though they were dang near ninety years old, they were managing for themselves, in their way, at their home. The house had a guestroom, but my old man said we would stay at a nearby motel. Since he was paying for this, I had no objections. He had been down there taking care of things before, so I figured he knew what he was doing, even if sometimes he acted a bit senile himself.

On the first day at their house, it started off normal enough. Grandma made breakfast. Afterward, I started working out in the yard, painting, cleaning, and sweating my butt off. It was summer in Southern Florida…duh…it is always summer there. As I had begun having heatstroke, thank goodness, it was time for lunch. It was not any cooler in the house, but after a gallon of iced tea, I figured I'd survive. Then it was back outside again until dinner.

Sometime after breakfast, the next day, I began noticing some very strange and bizarre behavior by my grandparents. Maybe their behavior was normal, how would I know. They were fixing little cat food dishes and setting them all over the house. The next thing I knew, I was up to my…er…in cats. At that moment, I had thought the awful odor was how old people smelled. It was, in fact, the aroma of tuna fish, cat piss, and crap, bottled up in a house for ten years with all the windows closed, baked by the sun without air conditioning, at temperatures over 110 degrees every day. If you don't clear your sinuses in an hour in that house, nothing else will. would if an hour in that house doesn't clear your sinuses.

Did I mention I am allergic to cats? That explained why my eyes had turned red and swollen shut. Soon after that, I was sneezing and coughing so badly that I had to spend the rest of my week outside, taking my meals under a palm tree.

Dad said there had to be over twenty-five house cats. No wonder the place smelled like someone crapped a carp! With that many critters, the litter box was certainly 'standing room only.' No kiddin', it was for certain kitties were doing their business in places they should not have been. If that weren't bad enough, Gramps would be outside feeding another thirty cats that lived on the property like an infecatstation.

Maybe they were being bussed in from the inner city for all I knew. I was in a sea of kitties when the plates touched the ground. For the record, I'm not crazy about one cat, and now I was in the middle of a freak'n catvention. It was catastrophic. Most of these animals looked like they'd been fighting in the MMA and mostly losing. There were some with catusions, catcussions, broken tails, and mange. What a pity; one kitty had an eyeball hanging out by a vein, and the rest looked like they could use a catscan.

After seeing that, I decided to skip lunch. Pop wasn't much of a cat lover either. He'd never go out of his way to hurt one, but he probably wouldn't run into a burning building to save one either. He was also complaining about the smell, the cost to feed them, and most of all, the cattations from the Health Department he had to answer. The city officials were having a catniption because of all the complaints from the neighbors.

Kitty lovers will argue that feeding and caring for a few felines is harmless, especially if it keeps the old folks busy and amused—and who doesn't want 'amused' old people? Besides the awful smell, all the cat food on the ground had increased the palmetto bug population in Gramp's backyard to just over the same number of people currently living in China. The principal difference is that bugs are much smaller than Chinese people so that you can keep millions of them in your backyard…bugs, that is…not Chinese people. Also, Chinese people do not run up your leg and try to nest in your shorts; it's only an assumption on my part but I only know one Chinese person, a young lady named Ping Pong. She never tried to climb up my leg, though; I think I would have liked that.

Besides crotch-nesting palmetto bugs, there were American, Asian, and German cockroaches, making Grandpa's backyard sort of a United Nations, of insects. I'm not an Entomologist (more of an Entenmann-ologist…love their donuts). When there are insects, there are predators. My Grandparents' double-lot in their residential sub-division had enough mice, rats, birds, lizards, frogs, and other insects, making it a half-acre version of the 'Wild Kingdom.' These insects are such a wonderful source of protein; it probably won't be long before someone comes out with a breakfast bar called. 'Palmetto Protein Bars,' covered in chocolate and coconut.' [Yum Yum] That is not the worst; these cats were nothing more than a mobile home for at least a trillion fleas and other virulent diseases.

With the potential of an outbreak of plague greater than that of the Middle Ages and me standing in the middle of it, when I made it back to the hotel, I took a bath in Lysol® and Clorox™. When I complained to my dad about the cats, he told me what he had done during his last visit.

"I figured out an ingenious way to get rid of most cats outside and a few inside. I passed out free tickets to the 'Garfield movie to all the kitties and had a mini bus waiting at the end of the block to take them to the theatre downtown. After the movie, the cats were told they would stop at Chucky Cheese for pizza before returning to the house. Instead, they were taken to the animal shelter. They promised me, after a week, if no one claimed them, they would be transferred to Homeland Security, deported to Tijuana, and sold to a 'Cat Juggling Ring.' While my plan had been very effective previously, this time, your Grandpappy is watching me like a hawk, constantly taking inventory of his kitties."

Gramps may have been old, but he was one crafty old coot. Every time the old man or I put up a poster in the neighborhood offering an all-expenses paid evening with dinner and tickets for the Broadway Show 'Cats,' Grandpa came behind us and tore them down. He was going to make sure we didn't kid-nap or cat-nap, any more of his pets by luring them away with cat-nip and free tickets.

While I loved my grandparents, I wasn't sorry when it was time to go home. I still smelled like a wet muskrat in heat, dragged through a city landfill, a week later. I tried licking myself clean, but I kept coughing up hairballs. I had to run through an automated truck wash at the Love's Moore Haven Truck Plaza as a final resort. The brushes stung a bit, especially on the naughty parts, but to tell the truth, I derived great pleasure during the hot wax and buff.

For those of you who think I have spent enough time talking about cats, all I can say is TOUGH KITTY. There should be a law against having even one cat, but I know women love them. As for you guys…and you know who you are, how can I say this and still be politically correct—if you happened to be 'manly challenged' go ahead and keep one or two little pussies, if that makes you feel 'purrrrrfectly' happy.

However, that brings us to the cataclysmic question of '…How many cats does a person need?' What is reasonable? There was an article in the 'Washington Post' by Leef Smith about an eighty-four-year-old woman who had to appear in court because she kept 488 cats in her townhouse. Yo…Spanky, if you own 488 cats, you probably don't have a freakin' idea what the word reasonable means. You probably don't even have a firm grasp on reality.

Besides all the previously mentioned problems I've mentioned about having too many cats, this lady's problem was even worse. According to the police report, 222 of the cats were already dead. While you would call that a catastrophe…I call it 'a good start.' One of the charges was that she had tried to obstruct justice when authorities came to her home while attempting to hide her pets.

Let me see if I got this right. You live in a townhouse, own 488 cats, and are trying to hide them from a court-ordered search? All right, I have a few ideas on how to hide the 222 dead ones, at least. I do not want to go into great detail, but it would involve a blender, a bucket, and a toilet. Disposing of the other 'live' 266 cats would be more difficult, though not impossible.

The court ordered a mental evaluation to see if the woman was insane. Hmm...do you think there was any chance of that? I'm sure my grandparents, like this old lady, started out with one cat. Then…what the heck, two cats, three cats, and the next thing you know, she was running a cat-house. I am highly confident this lady and my grandparents are not the only victims of this tragic illness.

What is the solution? [Don't try to steal this idea because there is a patent pending] I have designed a modified 'Cat Feeder' that can be installed wherever you have elderly people or anyone showing signs of 'Catafeedingtosis.' What ole Gramps and Granny don't know is that when a cat hops onto the feeder, sensors, not detecting any humans within the immediate area, becomes a Cat-a-pult. FLING…Weeeeeeee! The little freeloading fur-ball goes flying.

Not only will this teach the furry moocher not to come back for a second helping of Tender Vittles®, but you can also adjust the range and distance. This is where your military artillery experience would pay off. You can choose landing sites such as a trampoline, a swimming pool, a Doberman kennel, or a BBQ Grill. You never know…a whole business could develop with products like: Squirrel-a-Pult; Rat-a-Pult; Wife-a-Pult. Why the possibilities are endless. I hope to make enough money from this deal to start that group home for young foreign Asian female exchange students, like I've dreamed of…many nights.

Everyone is afraid of something. I'm afraid I will live so long, I'll be found walking around in a catatonic state feeding a cat…or cats, [the quantity is irrelevant]—any more than 'none' is too many. I imagine I'd also be wearing checkered Bermuda shorts, black socks with sandals, a Hawaiian shirt, a John Deere ball cap, and singing songs by Wham.

If I'm ever found in that condition, in the name of all that is holy, I'm begging you, grab a rock, a shovel, or a two-by-four, and immediately bludgeon me to death or call someone who will. Don't let me go on suffering like that.

Thanks, I know I can count on you.

Grizzly G. Gus © 2024

THE BAKE SHOP

Maeve chuckled as she fumbled for the key to unlock the front door of Maeve's Mostly Marvelous. Although hardly anyone now asked, "Mostly Marvelous WHAT?"

The response of "Why, whatever's here, of course!" always made her chuckle. Still smiling to herself she set the faded spell book carefully on the counter and opened it's somewhat yellowed pages. Ah! There it was! She had high hopes for this latest attempt. She would dearly love just a bit more sleep in the mornings and this would certainly help. As much as she loved running her own bakery shop, getting up so early just wasn't her thing. Mixing the ingredients, she took a deep breath, added just a pinch of bluong root, and chanted the brief rhyme.

"Rising fast…rising well…be the best bread…that ye may sell!". Lowering her arms she stepped back to wait. Just then she heard the rattle of keys in the lock, turning she blinked. "Janie? What are you doing here? Is everything alright at home?"

"Of course, sweetheart. But you forgot your lunch again." Her partner responded gaily holding out a small basket.

"You know you shouldn't work all day without food, it makes you grumpy. You know how…" she paused sniffing loudly.

"Oh my, that smells marvelous! You truly have a knack for this. Be sure to bring some home dear."

"Oh of course." Smiling fondly Maeve blew her a kiss. "And thank you so much for the food. You spoil me!"

"Not at all, sweetie. Well, I suppose I should get back, the garden isn't going to water itself!"

With a wink and a sidelong glance, Jane swept out the door, closing it gently behind her. Turning Maeve smiled happily at the sight of several perfectly risen bread loaves. It was going to be a great day!

Jeff Webber © 2024

THE GREATEST DAY IN MY LIFE

Set in the near future

Today is going to be a great day, quite possibly the best day of my life.

That might seem to be a bit presumptuous in a life well lived, and trust me, I have lived a full and great life, but I really think that this may be the very best. Today I will appear in a big budget (well medium budget anyway) horror movie, but more than that, a movie in a series that I have followed since the very first film came out way back in 2001.

The first film in the series was definitely not big budget. It looked like it was filmed on handheld cameras, maybe even on mobile phones, and there really wasn't much of a story line. Basically, it centered around a group of teenagers camping in the woods in the Midlands. They, of course, start arguing and one by one slowly disappear. It was really a copy (although they called it an homage) of many of the most famous movies of the genre, Halloween. Friday 13th, Nightmare on Elm Street and the countless others that started in the 1980's and seemed to go on forever.

What made this movie different though was that it was set in England, featured British actors and had very imaginative kills. It did have a kind of twist in the story line, in that you were led to believe that the teenagers were killing each other, subtle clues pointed at various members of the gang, but by kill 3, while the cast continued to suspect each other we, the audience, were introduced to the mystery killer.

Far from being the typical, hulking, gigantic killer of many films of the genre, we saw an average sized person, masked of course, in street clothes and armed with a large machete. There was no back story introduced, just the killer, stalking the kids one by one. Even when the kills were not completed by the large knife, such as a tree branch impaling or a fall to the death, the killer would approach the corpse and carve 5 lines into the body in the shape of a rudimentary star.

This led to the killer being referred to as the StarKiller in later movies, although the movie itself was called "Who Killed Barry?". Later this was changed to "Who the Fuck Killed Barry?". A line that was repeated several times in the film.

I watched this movie at a local cinema, it was half full and the floors were sticky with crushed popcorn and spilled soft drinks, but my attention was held, and I even found myself mentally cheering along as all of the teens gradually met their end in imaginative fashion.

However, something about the movie made it stand out for me (and for many others) and it was the incredible performance of the actor who played the killer. With no lines to speak, wearing a sweatshirt and jeans and a very nondescript mask that looked like a cheap Halloween alien, he had to really project to become interesting and even believable.

Not since Nick Principe's amazing performance as Chromeskull in "Laid to Rest" has an actor been more convincing. The scene where a frustrated Chromeskull shrugs and sighs at the fact that he has to try again to kill a victim was a genre defining moment and had the movie itself been better I am sure there would be a long series of movies in that franchise

The killer in "Who Killed Barry" seemed to ooze emotion and despite his lack of facial features through the mask, we managed to sense his frustration, his anger his glee at a job when finished and found ourselves almost understanding why he was doing his dirty deeds. Almost.

Many people stayed through the credits to see who had played this part and that's where the producers pulled a truly great stunt. The credits rolled on through, listing the characters and the respective actors and then finally came.

The Killer - played by himself

The movie critics both loved and hated this. Everybody had seen the brilliance of the performance in a halfway decent homage movie, and everyone wanted to know who had played the killer. The production company however remained tight-lipped.

This created a buzz that rivalled that surrounding The Blair Witch Project. Rumours that the Killer was actually a released murderer or a major screen actor that couldn't reveal his identity for contractual reasons and every possible scenario in between abounded.

The movie itself really didn't deserve the attention that it was getting (although in my mind the Killer's performance did) but once started it grew exponentially and soon even people outside of the movie's target audience knew of both the film and the rumours.

So, it was a given that a part 2 would be made.

With the buzz still around the studio announced "The Starkiller pt.2" as a shooting project and the internet again became full of rumours about who would play the Killer.

Damn, this bus feels like it is taking forever to get to the studio, but I am sure that's more my excitement than reality.

Anyway, they made a part 2 and the usual comparisons appeared in the reviews. The movie was declared "not as good as the original" and "Better than the original" and "a worthy successor to the original" all at the same time. Truth be told it was an okay movie, the performance of the Killer was just as good as in the first, the writing a bit pedestrian but at least with a bigger budget the production was more professional and the acting of a higher calibre.

The film beat all budget predictions however and the British audience lapped it up. It even made inroads into the American and European Markets and the writing was on the wall for the birth of a franchise. A bigger budget and better directing and production meant that the tension was dialled up in the film and the kills were fairly realistic.

This is where the Starkill franchise managed to ride the coattails of a changing trend in what could and couldn't be shown on the movie screen (and on tv). With the beheading scene in 1976's "The Omen" being the first fairly realistic decapitation in a major Hollywood movie, and certainly in any film starring such a major A List actor as Gregory Peck, the stage was set for more gruesome kills than had been previously seen.

However, once we entered the 2000s there were 2 fairly separate schools of special effects. Many mid to low budget movies continued using fairly basic gags, relying instead on the direction and editing to build up the excitement instead of using realistic effects.

A trend started by the original Friday 13th film where Tom Savini orchestrated the beheading of Betsey Palmer in a scene that if you "watch" carefully actually reveals a watch (not worn by the actress) a truly awful perspective problem and a distinct lack of realism was overshadowed by the "I did NOT see that coming" shooting of the scene, continued.

Many movies made the kills so unrealistic that audiences cheered at the cheesiness and Tom Savini became a legend. Though to be fair his skills as both an actor and a special effects guy improved exponentially, resulting in great performances in "From Dusk Till Dawn" and other films.

Some movies bucked that trend. The 'Final Destination' series had some great effects as did the "Saw" series (though those movies were hit or miss in terms of writing, production and directing) but generally the horror franchises and independent movies tended to stagnate in terms of realism.

The Starkiller franchise definitely upped their realism in the special effects department and even though sometimes the story lines were lacking and a couple of very dodgy collaborations with other franchises were attempted, the quality and realism of the effects carried the movies.

Another big problem affecting the movies was what started to be shown on Television. There was a huge rise in forensic and police procedural dramas such as "CSI", "Silent Witness", "NCIS" and others that started to show dissected bodies on the autopsy table. Open body cavities and A-List actors tended to normalize the horror element that many movies had relied upon for shock value.

Oh cool, the next stop is mine. I will get off the bus and take a short walk to the studio to check in. I still can't believe I will be in "Starkiller 12" which is only the working title, but damn! I am going to be in the movie!

So, back to the TV thing, if you can sit with your family at 8:00 pm and see an opened-up chest cavity, organs being removed and weighed, Y incisions being made on a corpse it becomes increasingly difficult to impress people in a movie where not so long ago such scenes would make you gasp in the cinema.

This franchise however achieved cult status by sticking to three principles, the quality and originality of the special effects during the kills, sticking to the stalk and slash roots of the genre and keeping the acting talent of the Killer consistent.

By the time the 7th movie in the franchise was released the killer was "unmasked' so to speak and revealed to be a solid working actor named Alan Ridge. He had just been in the right place at the right time to get the role in the first movie. Hoping to get more prestigious roles in the future he had asked for his name to be kept off of the credits, paving the way for one of the greatest promotional gags ever.

His talent was recognized and appreciated, and he stuck with the franchise that had been his bread and butter for years. He made a few other movies and worked the West End a few times, but he knew where his allegiance lay, and he has appeared in all the movies since the first when he was simply billed as "The Killer – Himself".

The trade press and websites sometimes ran articles wondering how they made the kills look so realistic, but it wasn't until the 10th movie that some tabloid rag of a newspaper revealed the secret and almost threatened the continuation of the franchise. However, after a lot of legal action and expenditure the series has continued and now... now I get my shot at appearing in the movie. This is my Bus Stop, time to get moving to the studio.

The walk to the studio is refreshing, a light breeze, clear skies and my excitement level is rising. Having checked in I go to the Green Room and wait, for what seemed like a long time but was probably no more than15 minutes. A smartly dressed intern comes to collect me and I am taken to an office to do "the paperwork".

Most of the paperwork was already done when I registered with the production company, I simply read through it to check its accuracy and initialled all the relative places to verify and then had to read through and sign a "hold harmless" waiver that was very much like the one that I signed when I made a tandem skydive some years ago. That was another thing on my bucket list to complete, but while thrilling, quite honestly being in this movie is so much better.

Then they asked me if I would like to meet Alan Ridge, The Killer. My answer? Not just yes but HELL YES!!!

So, I was taken back to a dressing room and after a knock on the door was escorted into the presence of one of the greatest actors in any horror franchise ever.

With his regular looks, slight stature and soft natural voice it was hard to believe that this man had scared literally millions of people, including me, and was the highest paid actor in horror history. The other big surprise was that he was just so nice. He put me at ease straight away and listened attentively as I gushed about what a huge fan I was.

He asked me if I was open to direction and told me that we would have a very quick rehearsal. He also said that I should react as much as possible, scream if it felt appropriate, yell, shout do whatever I thought was necessary, but more importantly just be natural. "Leave the acting to me" was his actual quote I believe. However, something I didn't realize was that if they actually used my voice in the production, I would get a 25% bonus (presumably as they wouldn't have to do any kind of voice over).

Apparently, I will be Victim #3 and I assured him this would be my honour. My height, general stature and looks resembled the actor playing the role that I would be the stand in for, but he wasn't available to see me right now.

Promising to meet me on the set, he took his leave and I was escorted back to the green room. I waited, excitement building and when someone knocked on the door and came in I was ready to go, but it was the production company's doctor.

He thoroughly checked my medical file, looked at my doctor's notes and performed an examination, quietly, calmly and with great professionalism. Honestly everything about this process was reassuring and professional. I thought back to the humble, low budget origins of the franchise and how professional and slick everything is now.

Finally, I was walked to the set. It was an indoor forest/woodland setting, incredibly realistic and well lit. If it wasn't for the stage lighting and the crew you would think you were outside, it was just that good. The director came over with Alan Ridge, who introduced us. I was so surprised when the director thanked ME for being a part of his film, I explained that as a long-time fan of the franchise the honour was all mine, but he insisted and shook my hand for a long time.

Alan Ridge smiled and promised to make the scene as good and as true to the franchise as possible as he walked me over to a large tree where I was to have my back to the camera. I will be bent over, looking at and picking mushrooms. He explained that he will appear in shot quickly and unknown to me. He will tap me on the shoulder with the tip of a very large knife and as I turn around, I should look as scared as possible as he grabs my hair and pulls my head back in preparation for the kill. I still couldn't believe my luck, this is my dream come true, meeting my acting hero and actually being in one of the most successful horror franchises of all time.

The director walked me over to the base of the tree, reaffirmed Alan's instructions and asked if I had any questions. Of course, I had hundreds but I simply asked where I was to be struck and he said that Alan improvises a lot based on the reaction of the stand in. "Just go with the flow and don't forget to feel free to yell, scream or even cry," if they could use my vocal track, he assured me they would and the money would go up by 25%.

So, it's time, I am here, standing by the tree. My back is to the camera and the director yells, "quiet on set, talent stand by, I need to take this shot in one".

"Is everybody ready and knows what to do? We are going in Five, Four, Three......."

I am so excited I am almost trembling, but I do what I was told, bend over and look at the mushrooms, I keep fake foraging until I feel that tap on the shoulder with the knife tip, shit that hurt a little and probably drew a little blood, but it's okay, it's worth it.

I slowly turn around and FUCK I was NOT prepared for how genuinely scary Alan Ridge is with the mask on, I see a look of cold disgust in his eyes, but I know that he is acting.

I have no choice; I scream loudly, and I know that I look terrified because I AM terrified. However, as Alan grabs my hair and pulls my head back with a sharp tug I am relaxing into the role a little.

Time seems to slow down for me, and I see his arm is going up high now. The light glints from the huge blade as he slams it down into my chest, there is a dull pain...

From the front page of the Daily Record... May 24th

We uncover the sick truth about the StarKiller Franchise

Are you one of the millions of people that like the Starkiller franchise of horror films? You won't be after you learn what we discovered about their so-called realistic death scenes.

While it is true that euthanasia or assisted suicide has been legal in the UK for a while now, most people have assumed that it was always in a calm, quiet and medical environment. However, the sick people at Starkill Productions have desecrated the sacred right of terminally ill people to die comfortably and calmly surrounded by their loved ones by using them in their disgusting movies.

Due to the ever-growing demand for greater realism this awful production company negotiated a secret deal with insurance companies and healthcare providers that we have spent months uncovering. Instead of faking the kills in these atrocious movies that pander to the lowest denominator they are paying off terminally ill patients and actually killing them on screen!

This newspaper was not prepared for this discovery, in fact several of our researchers walked off the investigation once it became clear that

Starkill was exploiting desperate people with terminal conditions by offering them money to be killed on camera!

So far we have not uncovered anything illegal about this horrendous scheme as everything appears to be with the patient/victim's full consent, but there is no doubt in the mind of this newspaper that it is immoral and exploitative.

The victims of this disgusting practice sign waivers that guarantee that their families and heirs will not sue the production company and a medical doctor, licensed in euthanasia practice, is always present at the filming.

We contacted Starkill Productions to ask them to attempt to justify this awful process but so far they have declined to comment, as has Alan Ridge the "Actor" that presumably perpetrates these atrocities, but we feel it is our duty to warn people that when you support and watch one of these movies, you are witnessing real murder and real killing and while you are not legally complicit in this process, morally you should be ashamed of yourself.

From Page 27 of The Daily Record, June 2nd

Correction

The national Record is instructed to issue an apology to Starkill Productions. There is no evidence of exploitation in their practice of filming the suicide of terminally ill patients and this new3spaper was wrong to use the word "murder". Instead, the term "assisted suicide" should have been used.

While this newspaper still condemns this practice, we had no intention of maligning the character of anyone associated with Starkill Productions.

We understand that the actor Alan Ridge holds a medical diploma in Euthanasia Practice and works in conjunction with a medical doctor on all such scenes.

Excerpt from an online blog

The Reel Truth Blog – January

With the story written by the "journalists" of the National Recorder that The Starkiller Franchise actually uses terminally ill patients in their movie kills it was feared that the franchise might be forced to end. However, we have discovered that after months of legal wrangling and a settlement of an undisclosed amount paid by the "newspaper" to the production company the franchise will continue. In fact, the receipts for "Stalker in the Woods" the 12th film in the franchise are predicted to be double the take of the previous films in the franchise as people flock to see for themselves what all the fuss is about.

Peter Draper © 2022

HOMECOMING

Home is where the heart resides, or so I've heard them say.
I never knew just what that meant until I went away.
I've travelled 'round this wide brown land just like a rolling stone
And never seen a place quite like the one that I call home.

I've walked on beaches pure and white that gleamed beneath the
sun,
I've swum in oceans deep whose beauty cannot be outdone.
I've see the heart, so red and stark, so desolate and dry.
The Great Outback, the dusty track, the blinding, vivid sky.

On mountain peaks I've stood amid the rocks and dazzling snow.
By rivers, lakes, and forests deep, where men so rarely go.
I've fished in waters few have seen, sat silent in the bush serene
observed by none 'cept Nature while I watched the flowers grow.

In busy cities, hours I've spent, alone amongst the throng
of madding crowd and traffic loud where no sane thing belongs.
I've walked the streets in darkness sometimes fearful for my life
Thinking every stranger held a gun, a cudgel, or a knife.

I've made some pals and possibly some enemies as well.
Will they all miss me when I'm gone? I really cannot tell.
Celebrities? I've known a few. Some even called me 'Friend'.
Perhaps in sport, it matters nought, time levels in the end.

So now at last I'm turning home to satisfy the need

To visit places long remembered, friends so long unseen.

Some will be there, some will be gone, some passed away, some just
moved on,

Life's fickle finger guides us on to where we need to be.

Thomas Greenbank © 2024.

TRUTH AND FIRE

I have always found honesty in the flames. The light writhes between the soft plumes of smoke and ash, performing scenes of knowledge and wisdom. It is most mornings that my eyes itch from soot and truth.

If anything, truly starts, this story begins, much like the children themselves, with their mother. A thin slip of a creature, barely more than a child herself, and with no business this deep into the forest that night, nor any other. Whether it was love or duty that brought her to me, the fires did not reveal, but they did show her desperation to give her husband children. And so, I was ready when she rapped on the door to my hut, despite the hour.

"No, girl. I won't help you," I answered from my chair and the warmth of my hearth.

"Please, my mother told me stories about you. I have nowhere else to go." She leant, tired, against my closed door.

"Nonsense. The world is large, you have countless wheres to go."

"Nowhere that can help me. Only you, Mother Mandrake. Please."

If I'm honest, and before the flames I can be naught else, it was the respect in her plea that pulled me from my chair. It had been so long since someone had spoken to me with any reverence. I opened the door for her, "Come in, then. I will mix it for you."

She paused a moment, her eyes wide, but bowed her head as she spoke. "Of course, you know already."

"I know. I know that lump of a woodsman lays with you each night, dropping his worthless coins into your purse. Currency that can purchase no babe."

"Oh, I assumed…"

"Of course you did. But no, the draught is for him to drink."

I saw it then, a spark of something. More than determination or strength. I eyed her as I ground at my large stone mortar. She sat silently, but the reflection of my hearth's light danced in her eyes. It was faint, but the fire's power whispered in her blood.

"It will give you no happiness," I declared, as I gave her the vial.

"Thank you, Mother Mandrake." And with that, she fled back into the night.

My words were unkind, and inaccurate. She did have happiness, four years of it. Soon after her visit, she brought twins into the world. A boy, Henri, and a girl, Giselle. Four years of challenges, meagre suppers, fatigue, and joy. She loved her babes, and they returned that love, but she never truly recovered from the difficulties of pregnancy and labour. In the fourth year, the winter claimed her.

The woodcutter, who had struggled while she lived, floundered with her gone, and did what any fool man would do. He brought the wrong woman into his home to help him care for the children. A woman with plans to fill their beds with babes of her own, if only those beds were empty. It took her a few years and some harsh seasons, but her dark whispers slid through his ears, and one day their father took Henri and Giselle into the woods to look for berries.

Giselle told her brother that she had heard the woman scheming at night. She bade Henri to bring his sack of skimming pebbles with him. When moonlight came to the clearing and their father had not returned, they looked for their path home. It was only then Henri revealed that, jealously protective of his stones, he had instead been marking their journey with crumbs he'd gathered from the cabin floor. Crumbs that had long since been eaten by the birds of the forest.

It was another two days before my flames danced the children into my sight. By this time they were huddled together against a tree, their arms wrapped tight and numb around each other.

I flew from my hut with as much haste as my ageing limbs would allow. Dawn was teasing the sky by the time I found them. Their breaths were slow and barely made steam, but I roused them. I tempted them back to the world with barley sweets and some gingerbread I had with me, promising that and more if they could will their frozen frames to follow me. The boy sank more deeply against the trunk on an elm, sucking the sugar in his dry mouth, and I feared I'd still lose them there. But his sister met my eyes and forced herself to stand. It took three more pieces of gingerbread, but by noon I had them in front of my stove, asleep, with dribbles of mushroom soup on their chins.

Henri woke first. His widening eyes absorbed the sights of my hut, including me working my pestle against some lichen and dewberries. He scuttled backwards into a corner, knocking over a broom and bucket in his scramble. The clattering awoke his sister, and she too soaked up her surroundings. She looked up at me, her chin firm against her obvious fears.

"Are you going to eat us, witch?"

I held back my smile, as it may have contradicted my denial. "No, Giselle, I'm not going to eat you."

"How do you know my name?"

"I knew your mother. She sat where you now sit and asked for my help."

"She's lying!" Henri had found his voice.

"No, she's not," Giselle responded. "We've been asleep here for hours. If she wanted us for meat, we'd be meat.

"Good girl." I allowed the smile to peek. "Now, get up. That soup is the last free meal you'll have from me."

"You're going to kick us out?" Henri squeaked.

"That'd make a waste of my day, wouldn't it?" I replied. "No, you can stay here as long as you like. I'll house you, feed you, care for you, but you'll work for it."

"No," grunted Henri. "We should go back to the clearing and find our way home."

"Our way home?" Giselle gasped, "Father left us out there to die!"

"You don't know that!" Henri turned his head away, unable to meet her eyes, "He could be out there looking for us right now."

"He won't be, Henri. I told you what I heard. That woman wants us dead and he agreed."

Henri clutched himself with folded arms and looked down at his feet.

Giselle tuned to me. "We'll stay, if you'll have us."

And that was that.

They spent the afternoon clearing out a corner of my hut and laying down some bedding, before busying themselves with the evening work that was always needed. I stayed at my stove, lost in both the flames and my own thoughts.

"I'm sorry for earlier."

I blinked out the sparks and turned to face her. "For what, girl?"

"For being rude. For calling you a witch."

"I'll take the apology for the first, but you're right about the second."

Her eyes widened, reflecting the light of my stove. I met them, waiting for her response to my honesty.

"What should we call you?"

"I don't know. Your mother called me Mother Mandrake when she came here."

"I don't think Henri will want to call you Mother… but if our mother did perhaps… Grandmother? Baba?"

"Baba. Fine."

And again, that was that.

\#

Winter left and returned, and what had started out strange had become our every day. Our home was crowded, and there was never too much, but there was enough. I was sitting by my window, wondering about the chances of an early thaw, when Giselle pressed a warm cup into my hand.

"Tea, Baba."

"Thank you, my dear. Come, sit with me."

She drew a stool up beside my chair.

"Wasn't your brother supposed to sweep this morning, not you?"

She hesitated a moment. "He says it is a woman's task. That it is better for him to do the more difficult man's work of collecting wood or water. He's off fetching a bucket from the stream, now." she added, too quickly.

I snorted. Far more likely that he was asleep under our very feet, nestled in the warmth of the chicken coop caged between the short stilts of my hut. But he kept my fires well fed with more wood than I could collect without him. And his troubles were her truth to find, not mine to tell.

"Has… has the fire said anything about my father?" The look on her face reminded me how young she was.

"The flames do not speak to me, they show me things. But no, they have not shown me of your father."

"Oh. So… it doesn't talk?"

"Not to me." I decided it was time. "But it speaks to you?"

She nodded. "I think it told me what father and that woman were going to do."

"The flames give truth to those who can see it, or hear it."

"But what good is it? We were still left in the woods."

"That's not the flame's fault though, is it? You just trusted the wrong person to help you."

"But he's, my brother."

"Yes, but a man is less his blood and more his deeds."

She mused for a moment. "He didn't really believe me, that's why he didn't bring his precious skimming stones. I think part of him still doesn't believe Father left us. Or at least doesn't want to believe it."

"That's the thing about the truth, Giselle. You have to have the courage to stare right into it."

"And then it can't hurt you?"

"Oh, no. Truth is fire. It can always hurt you. But best to see it coming, no?"

I left her there and went outside to cast food to the chickens as loudly as I could.

\#

More seasons came and went, and years of watching the flames finally left their mark on my sight. Much of my world was shadow now, and I relied on smell, and sound, and touch to get by, such as caraway seed being ground in my mortar or the bubbling of soup come to a boil.

Even the children's growth towards adulthood was known more to me by the thickness of the hands and wrists when I held them.

The morning chores accounted for, and once Henri was safely out on one of his long walks, Giselle joined me by the fire. As I stared into the light, she closed her eyes to listen. It had become our private communion. Today, for the first time since I took the twins into my home, the flames revealed their old cabin to us.

"He's alone. She has left him."

"Yes," I agreed. "Have you heard why?"

"I think… yes. She could not bear him children."

"That's what they thought," I concurred. "But he could not give them to her. Not without the help your mother sought from me."

"Oh." She listened longer. "And then his guilt about us turned ugly and they fought and… she left."

The fire showed me a portion more than that, of drunken rage and blackened eyes, but I spared her from it.

"And now he is alone."

"What did you do to him, witch?" An adolescent voice shouted from the door.

We had been so caught up; we hadn't heard Henri return.

"I knew it! You cursed him didn't you!"

"No, Henri, it's not like that!" Giselle ran to her brother's side.

He shoved her to the floor and, looming over her, spat out his words. "And you, you sit at her side as she hexes your family? When she finishes with Father, am I next? So, she can have you all to herself?"

"Baba loves us, Henri. She cares for us as if we were her own. Feeds us, clothes us, houses us!"

"You mean she's trapped us. Made us slaves! I bet she made Father walk us into the woods that day!"

I should have held my tongue. Should have. "There's no lock on this cage, boy."

He stared at me, over his sister, then turned and fled.

Giselle watched him leave. She came to my side and took my hands in her trembling ones.

"Good luck, my child. Look after yourself."

I felt her tears fall on my forearms, and then I was alone in the hut.

I sought solace in my hearth. The fire's light cast away the clouded shadows on my eyes and showed the twins moving through the forest. My failing sight had kept me from seeing them clearly for over a year. They looked so much like the man and woman they would soon become. No longer small, frightened children, they worked their way through the wilderness to tamer woods and they found the old cabin that must have seemed so much smaller to them now.

They met their father as he pulled his hand wagon with his day's lumber. All three dissolved to tears as they clung to each other. I hoped against hope and watched as they supped on broth and bread. But as the moon rose high, and their father shared some brandy with his returned son, the whispering began.

The flames showed me the tale they spun while Giselle slept. Of a witch who lured the children away from their home. Who locked them in a cage and forced them to work for her, while also fattening them for slaughter. I saw their plan to bring the village to my home, with torch, axe, and rage. They would not find me easy prey. Age had pilfered from my body, but not my mind, not my power. I turned from my hearth to begin the work.

But then a curious gust rushed down my chimney and my fire flared into hectic action. Before my eyes, the frenzied lights played out the future before me. The village men, angry and fearful, would drink in Henri's tale. The mob would force its way through the forest towards my home as Giselle followed, pleading with her father to stop.

At my door, I saw myself standing defiantly, as I had planned, in front of the mass of ignorance and hate, ready to unleash my fury. But before I could act, Giselle would throw herself forward. She would hold herself firm in their faces and speak the truth, fearlessly. Words of rescue and of haven, a denial of capture and servitude. The crowd would turn to Henri. Caught between his father and his sister, the boy could only do the inevitable. He would call her out as a witch, her soul be shadowed by my own darkness. Despair would overcome my resolve, and I would falter as the men surged forward. I wrenched my eyes away before the flames could show her burning beside me.

For the first time in almost a century, fear infused me. Was this the future I had coming? A child burning at my side for the sin of loving me?

The flames showed the truth, and I had the courage to stare right into it. I could not fight. I could not flee. Only one thing could save Giselle. It would hurt, but before fire and truth, I would be fearless.

Before my resolve faltered, I knocked the stone guard free from the hearth. The fevered wind blew spark and ember into my home, igniting the dried herbs and old wood. The fire blazed and I gave myself to it. Through the agony, I thought of her, and how the fire spoke to her.

I willed myself to think of the future. After the flames claimed me and the pain had gone; when the wicked tales had been spun, corrupting my truth into terrible fable. I willed my spirit into the flames so it could be my voice she heard in the hiss of the oven and the pop of the embers. I would tell her I had no regrets. That I loved her. And I would help her to stare into the truth and stand before it. Fearless.

Mark Kramarzewski © 2024

JARHEAD JESS

At the end of my fourth month at Student Company (and the fourth week after I should have graduated), I was inserted into the next group of students. The first two classroom portions went by quickly, and I soon found myself back in the photojournalism class that I had previously failed. This class was directed by an instructor from the Navy, and she made photography much less intimidating.

However, on the day our partners were assigned, I was told that mine would be a female Marine Corps sergeant. Not only did this mean no goofing off, but there was no way I could have a pinch of Kodiak around her. The Marines all knew that we weren't supposed to be using tobacco, and I knew for a fact that a Non-Commissioned Officer (NCO) was not going to tolerate it.

This marine was an imposing woman, too. She was only three or four inches shorter than I was, but she was built like an athlete. You could tell that she could hold her own in a hand-to-hand combat situation, probably with several people simultaneously. She was the type of soldier who made you glad you weren't fighting for the other side.

Our first few assignments went by quickly and with minimal verbal exchange. Each day we were taught a photography technique and then sent to the campus grounds to apply it. These were essentially assignments that were done individually, so there seemed little point in assigning partners other than accountability.

I was rigid when I was around my partner. She rarely spoke and seemed to be very severe with her Marine Corps subordinates. More than once, she stopped what she was doing to force a couple of privates to do push-ups. I figured it was only a matter of time before I would be in the same position.

In the second week of photography class, I finally had to break down and ask my partner a question. She smiled sympathetically as I stammered.

"You can call me Jess," she said.

This, of course, was against the rules. Not only was she a sergeant, but I was still in training. You do not call a superior by their first name under any circumstances. This kind of infraction, no matter how trivial it may seem, can earn a soldier an enormous upbraiding.

I felt she was trying to reach out, but I politely refused. She then told me I could call her 'Sarge,' and we settled on that. Sarge was almost as serious of an infraction, especially to a member of the Marine Corps; but I accepted the olive branch, consequences be damned.

Jess turned out to be pretty cool. She always made good grades on her assignments, and through her personal tutelage, I was finally able to learn how to operate the same camera that I was beginning to believe had thwarted me. She would even let me take a pinch of Kodiak in her presence, provided we were far enough away from the school.

How did she find out? Well, as it turns out, Hanson and I were not as subtle as we thought.

As far as Marines go, my photography partner remains one of the coolest I have ever met. I'm not often wrong when it comes to being a judge of character, but this was one of those times when I was very glad to be wrong.

*****

One day, we were given an assignment to photograph each other. In this exercise, we were expected to demonstrate a camera technique known as "depth-of-field." This technique is supposed to bring detail from the foreground and the background into the photo. Although I may not even be describing it correctly, it was no less a difficult technique to learn.

We toyed with shots all morning until we broke for lunch. An examination of our photos when we returned to school revealed that we had finished our assignment early, so Jess proposed that we take a few humorous photos.

For the duration of our partnership, we never told jokes. Therefore, when she spoke of doing something humorous, I had no idea what kind of a sense of humor a person like that could have. However, this was my chance to try and get away with something, so I decided to say one of the goofiest things I could think of:

"You should photograph me in a bed of flowers."

"Okay," she replied without hesitation.

"Really?"

"Yeah. Let's go do it." She began walking. I followed her to a large bed of flowers outside the school, where she told me to lie down. She was either setting me up for big trouble or I had genuinely underestimated my photography partner.

"Hurry up. Get down there." She ordered.

Not one to back down from such an absurd order, I did as I was told. I lay amongst a beautiful arrangement of flowers, carefully inserting myself so as not to destroy them, then crossed my legs behind me and put my head in my hands, gazing thoughtfully outside the photo.

Click

Holy shit. Had we just done something humorous? We giggled, then ran upstairs to the computer lab to see what we had done.

Impressed beyond my wildest imagination, I sent the image to the printer. What I had done was risky business. This waste of school resources would not only be frowned upon but more than likely reported to my drill sergeants. However, I agreed to all the consequences the moment I lay down in that bed of flowers, so why not have a souvenir?

Much to my dismay, a Marine Corps gunnery sergeant met me at the printer. He was frowning and motioned for me to come over to him.

He was holding the photo.

"What kind of shit is this?" The gunnery sergeant demanded. His face was red, and a bead of sweat had begun to trickle down his temple.

I said nothing. What could I say? I stood there dumbly, waiting to have my neck snapped, a heart attack, or to be raptured.

"Who's your damn partner? Are you with Hanson again?"

I gasped and swallowed hard. He already knew who I was. That was REALLY bad.

"Negative, gunnery sergeant," I said once I finally remembered how to speak.

"Then who took this f*cking photo?"

I said nothing, but he followed my eyes as I slowly turned my head and looked at my partner. She was smiling.

The gunnery sergeant's angry face became twisted with confusion. I could see the struggle in his eyes as I tilted my head ever-so-slightly to see his reaction.

I could practically hear the internal dialogue. There was no way that a member of his United States Marine Corps could ever stoop to such a shenanigan!

Especially a SERGEANT in his United States Marine Corps!

After a few moments of mulling, it over, he shoved the photo into my chest and ordered me to sit down. I did as I was told, but when I got to my desk, the gunnery sergeant was still staring in bewilderment in my direction.

76

Peter McCollum   ©   2024

CRAZY BOB AND THE CHAIN GANG

Crazy Bob, that's what everyone called him, behind his back, had been continually inviting me to come out to his place in the country. He was my former boss before he moved back to Pennsylvania from Florida. A year later, I found myself living in Pennsylvania as well.

There was a long weekend coming up. It was either visiting Bob or putting the contents of my refrigerator in alphabetical order. Bob won by a slim margin. With a pocket full of change for the tolls, thirty pages of directions from Bob, a compass, and an Indian guide, we set out to explore the wilderness like 'Martin and Lewis,' 'Abbott and Costello, or more closely, the Lone Ranger and Tonto.'

The directions were very detailed. Bob, extreme in everything he did, named all the landmarks I would see on the four-hour trip…every MINUTE! The IHOP, Howard Johnson's, and Cracker Barrel were listed in his directions. When he estimated the time the trip would take from my home to his, he had not anticipated I would stop at each one. Due to my appetite, this trip was going to take days. Another reason would be because my Indian guide, 'Running Water,' had to stop and take a leak every thirty minutes.

"Have you ever heard of 'Tunkhannock, Pennsylvania? According to the map, we have to travel through there."

"Yes," grunted Running Water.

"Tunkhannock, that sounds like an Indian name…do you know what it means?"

"It means, 'Lotsa luck finding Bob's place, without me, paleface.'"

I was getting concerned as we had not passed a McDonald's or a Seven-Eleven in over twenty minutes. We truly had left civilization and were deeply thrust into the wilderness. There were no more signs of civilization. After another hour, right after Running Water's sixteenth rest stop, I was beginning to have a Big Mac attack.

Bob wasn't called 'crazy' without good reason. The directions he gave me were proof of that. For example. '…Turn left at an apple orchard, go over a bridge that used to be there, and go straight when you come to the cows in the pasture.' It continued, 'When you come to a fork in the road…take it.' Bob thought of everything, even adding, '…if you get to the place where you are totally lost, go back to where you know where you was. Then start over again and don't do the same thing as you had previously done.' I did get hopelessly lost and, in fact, went back to where I was sure of where I was. Thank goodness there was a Stuckey's, as I was down to my last five-pound salted pecan nut roll.

After getting gas and putting fuel in my car, I took off again. A while later, I started looking for a place to pull over so Running Water could take one of his frequent potty breaks. I discovered I accidentally left with my 'injun' still running in the bathroom stall at Stuckey's.

I could have gone back, but without all the rest stops, I could take days off my trip. I continued my trek all alone. With only Bob's directions to guide me, I felt very confident…I would die somewhere along the highway, where they would find my emaciated, shriveled, dehydrated corpse, hunched over the steering wheel, with Bob's bogus directions still clutched in my fist.

Call it fate or blind luck; I came to the end of everything at a lonely crossroad with a single building on the corner. It was a restaurant called the 'Better Than Nothing, Bar and Grill." As I was about to walk in, something caught my attention. It was a small cemetery on the side of the building were chiseled on one of the gravestones it read: 'I don't recommend the special.' Having lost my appetite, I continued down a paved road until the pavement stopped and a path continued.

Traveling on a winding, twisting, bumpy dirt road, not even passing a farmhouse for miles. I was so deep in the woods that I had to stop a bear and ask it for directions, which cost me a five-pound salted pecan roll. Eventually, I came to the end of the trail and my patience. Without any sign of the existence of another human being…I knew I was very close to Bob's home. He was not antisocial; he just had no use for people. That should have given me a clue of what he thought about me.

In utter frustration, I exited the car, knelt, and looked toward heaven for directions. I wasn't praying…Bob's house was on top of a mountain, so I figured it would be easier to see it that way. Sure enough, perched precariously atop a summit directly in front of me was a house fitting his description. Knowing where the home was…did not make getting to it any easier. Stretched across a gravel road was a cable with a sign that read, 'DON'T CARE WHO YOU ARE, KEEP OFF MY PROPERTY.' Yup, no mistake, this had to be his place. After re-attaching the cable, I threw the car's transmission into 'D' for Dang; this road is steep! Starting the ascent, I climbed so high I saw mountain goats wearing oxygen masks. Twisting, turning, and always winding higher, fighting off the altitude sickness…emerging from a low-level cloud, there was a two-story brick home. Bob had said I should make myself at home if he were not around. That probably did not include eating all his food, piling dirty dishes in the sink, throwing all my clothes on the floor, and scattering his records and tapes everywhere. You don't even want to know what I did in his bathroom. I'd just finished messing up the last closet when Bob and his brother Richard came in. After Bob made me clean up the house and put everything back, he suggested I change my clothes before he showed me around his property.

As we started down a path, I began to hear the sound of dueling banjos, and suddenly, Bob and Richard were standing in front of me, dressed in bib overalls, laughing, drooling, and holding rifles on me while Robert put shackles around my ankles.

'Billy,' Bob started pacing back and forth, quoting, '…You'll get used to wearing them chains after a while but never stop listening to them clinking. They'll remind you of what I've been saying for your own good. What we've got here is a failure to communicate.' You're here to build a road."

"I thought you invited me to the country for a relaxing weekend of masculine camaraderie, bonding, and maybe even a few grilled bratwursts thrown in."

"Well, you thought wrong, lard butt. Just think of this like a fat farm 'cause I'm gonna knock at least fifty pounds off ya before long." Bob let out with a wicked hillbilly laugh. "There ain't going to be no bonding or tree-hugging or any other touchy-feely crap like that. You want to bond with something…here's a shovel."

When I first met Bob in Florida, he was an up-tight dictator director in a coat 'n tie, speaking with a slight Pennsylvanian accent. Now he and his brother had turned into characters out of 'Deliverance,' complete with a southern drawl. With a pick 'n shovel and wheelbarrow, I was marched into the woods. There, I was forced to dig ditches, break rocks, and shovel dirt until my blisters had blisters. Bob was dancing a jig and singing about all the free labor he was getting to build his road. He boasted how this wasn't the first time he had captured unsuspecting hikers who had stumbled onto his land, making them work for him.

I asked him, "What do you think the authorities would say if they knew what you were doing up here."

"Doing what?" He asked innocently.

"You know, inviting people here with the expectation of a fun-filled weekend but then subjecting them to physical hardships."

"Ah, quit your whining; you're so fat; tying your shoes is a physical hardship, you blimp."

"Maybe…but what about the fun you promised? I'm not having any."

"Oh, why didn't you say so? I can fix that immediately. Would you like to play 'Hide and Seek?'"

"Uh-huh," I said before realizing who I was talking to.

Bob lowered his shotgun toward me and suggested, "Best run and hide, then." Fleeing through the wood like a convict, I heard his two vicious Dobermans in the distance.

Several hours later, after Bob finished his nap, he called off the beasts, allowing me to climb down from the tree.

"You want to play any other games?" Bob asked.

"What did you do with the other people?"

"Do you see any other remains…er…I mean, evidence?" He had a good point. It would be hard to find a body since he owned the whole mountain. As far as evidence…are chipmunks carnivorous?

The sun had already set when Richard announced it was quitting time. "You might as well stop now; it's so dark I'm afraid if I had to shoot you, I'd miss and hit some helpless fuzzy forest creature." It had been a long time since I had physically worked this hard. Actually, I had never worked this hard. This was probably why I no longer had the will to live or the strength to trudge up to the house. The dullard brothers tried to lift me into the back of their 'one-ton' pick-up, but I made it sink down into the mud. They would have left me tied to a tree all night, but with so much road work left, they couldn't afford to take the chance I wouldn't be eaten by a pack of coyotes or a horde of bloodthirsty chipmunks. There was no choice…maybe there was, but 'Dumb and Dumber' hooked me to the bumper and dragged me up to the house. I didn't object until a tree branch got lodged in my butt.

Bob was cooking dinner. Richard staked me outside so he could hose me down. After the delousing, we all sat down to dine. Bob may have been a crazed lunatic—but he knew how to cook. He kept taking swigs of his corn liquor and giggling all evening about the free labor he was getting until he had to go out and hunt down a moose just to finish filling me up. After dinner, the 'Brothers Grim' carried me to the shed in a wheelbarrow and locked me in for the night. I was so tired; I was asleep before my head could hit the pillow…if they had given me one, that is.

Sunrise found me '♫ On the Road Again ♫'…building it! While this wasn't what I was expecting when I accepted the invitation to visit Bob for the weekend, on the positive side, if I was ever to apply for a position on a chain-gang with the Georgia State Correctional Institute, at least I would have work experience.

Around noon, only Richard was guarding me as I finished my fifteenth chorus of '♫Swing Lo, Sweet Chariot ♫' Crazy Bob must have been off somewhere molesting a woodchuck. I convinced Richard to unchain me long enough to relieve myself. When it was safe, I made a break for it. I reached my car before being apprehended. I did not want to attract attention, so I just let my car roll down the hill without starting the engine. I left my luggage…reasoning, 'My life was worth more than a three-pack of BVDs, a tube of Preparation-H, and the rubber sheets my mom always made me take whenever I slept over at anyone's house.'

As my car gained speed, I whizzed past Richard, or rather, I whizzed on Richard, as I was still in the process of relieving myself. He just stood there with his toothless, wide-open mouth. Just as I was about to relax, I came around the bend at the bottom of the mountain…only to find Bob's truck blocking my escape and Bob aiming his rifle at me. I slammed on the brakes.

"Hi, Bob," I stammered.

"Just what do ya think yer doing?"

My mind began racing, thinking of a convincing lie he would buy. "Uh…well…you see…we…um…ah…ran out of rocks, yeah that's it. Richard said I should go into town to get some." I couldn't believe it when Bob moved his truck, unlocked the gate, and waved me through. Just as I was about to pass…he jumped in front of my car with his pistol drawn.

"Hold it right thar city slicker; you must think I'm pretty gall-darn stupid." I just looked at him blankly, imagining myself back in chains, digging ditches. "You can't get no rocks without no money. Dem rocks don't grow on trees, ya know." He stood there for a moment, looking at me with his beady little eyes and rubbing his chinless jaw. Then he handed me a hundred dollars and told me to pick out good ones. "Hurry back," he called, "cause you've got a lot of road to build, and the time is shorter than you." [laugh] [chuckle] [snort]

I know what you are thinking, '…How could anyone be so stupid?' You've got to understand ole Bob had been subjected to many years of training, like me, by the U.S. Military. That probably also explains why I went to town, bought the rocks, and spent the rest of the weekend…building his road.

M. David Lutz © 2024

THE MISSION

As darkness faded into light, I could just distinguish my landing place as a vacant alleyway. I watched as shadows turned into the stark sides of buildings, windows, doors and garbage bins. Perfect. Out of sight and secure. When it was light enough, I checked my Space-Time Locator to make sure the co-ordinates were correct. They were. I checked the date and time: 0910 hours, 3rd October 2013. My time was limited, I estimated I had just less than an hour to make things right. As soon as I had fully materialised, I pulled my laser from my pocket and marked a cross on the brickwork beneath my feet, then headed out of the alleyway into a busy street.

The constant whirring of the traffic, the smell of the exhaust fume, the bustling crowds and flashing neon lights of the city were unfamiliar to me. Where I had come from there was no need for such archaic forms of transport and most of the time people spent their nights in virtual worlds. Still, I found it rather exotic as I jostled my way along the hectic sidewalk. I quickened my step as I remembered the seriousness of my mission. I also recalled for a moment, the life I had just left behind, the course of which I was now attempting to reverse. All my previous attempts had failed. I had not been able to go back far enough. This time, having made it, it had to be done.

When I glances around, I realised I need not have worried about looking out of place. I was amazed at the variety and styles of attire of the people in the street. My tall slender body dressed in a white triellic jumpsuit probably looked no stranger than many of those who passed me by. I also wondered whether any of them could possibly imagine how science was about to change everything, not only their access to resources but by the genetic manipulation of the population in order to make everyone uniform in a quest to create the perfect human being – strong and healthy, resilient bur obedient and controllable.

I heard a crackling sound and felt a quiver beneath my feet.

"Hey, man, did you feel that?" a passerby asked as he grabbed me by the arm. I shook him free. I didn't reply but knew exactly what it meant: my time in the past was starting to run out. I quickened my step once more until I came to the right street where I interrupted a couple standing in a doorway.

"Excuse me," I began as I pulled the key from my jacket pocket and read aloud from the tag on the back. "159 Regent Street. Unit 4C. Is this the apartment block?"

"Yes. That would be the basement apartment, down there," the young woman said pointing to a door beneath street level. "I don't think there's anyone home though. It looks empty," she added politely.

I scurried down the nearby set of stairs after thanking the young woman and stood at the door, key in hand. I thought it rather curious that Professor Dalton had kept the key all these years. Perhaps deep down he had an inkling of what was to come. I won't be home. Use the key, but make it look like a break-in, he had told me when we first met. Then take the report from the briefcase and destroy it. It may not stop it completely being developed but will definitely slow it down. He may now be 91 years old and a bit physically frail, but he still had his wits about him, I mused.

The key turned effortlessly, and I cautiously stepped inside. It was dark and dingy, but I didn't want to turn any lights on, but I didn't want to turn any lights on in case it attracted attention. The briefcase was easy to find, leaning against his desk in the study. I check inside and pulled out a neatly bound wad of paper that looked like a first draft. I ran my finger across the title on the cover page – The Genetic Modification of the Human Species by Professor J Dalton.

Before I had a chance to trash the place, as instructed by the Professor I heard and felt another crackling. It was now definitely time to get a move on, so I ran out and up the stairs clutching the report tightly under my arm. After a brief survey up and down the street to see if I was still undetected, I raced back to the alleyway, zigzagging my way through the oncoming pedestrian traffic.

You're the perfect person for the job. It should be seamless if you follow my instructions, Professor Dalton said at our second meeting about a month ago. Since hearing of your time travel missions into the past I had to see if you could do it for me. I really want this done so I can die with a clear conscience. The mistakes we make…without knowing the possible repercussions. It's now time to set things right. Are you sure you are not GM? he asked me for the last time, just before I left. Because if you are…well you know what that would mean," he added.

"Yes. I am sure I'm not GM," I lied once again as I really wasn't sure.

As soon as I reached the alleyway, I threw the report into one of the garbage bins, followed by the key. I set it alight with my laser. Now it was time to head home. When I got back, if I got back, I would be content knowing I had done something positive for the future of humanity, despite possible consequences. I stood as still as I could on the cross I had marked earlier. Then, as I watched the flames dance high in the bin, I typed the homeward bound settings into the keypad on my belt, pressed the start button and felt my body disappear back into the darkness again.

Jenny England © 2024

DREAMING OF CUSTARD

I am living for the day when I realise
that i don't hate you anymore. maybe,
it will happen in the silence of the custard
my spoon opening up a yellow void
and finding nothing beneath but an emptiness
that once overflowed with the green acid bile
of fury only just suppressed and now rendered
soft and creamy — not quite like the milk of human
kindness but with a blessed blandness that releases me
from a sleepless night into the fresh, sun-touched golden
tongue-licking mellowness of a first hate-free day.

Prompted by Ali Whitelock's poem 'in the silence of the custard' from her collection 'The Lactic Acid in the Calves of Your Despair', Wakefield Press, Adelaide, 2020

Maree Gladwin © 2024

THERAPY

It was a cool and windy afternoon. From time to time, I could hear the roar of the clouds that threatened rain. The black can can tights under the grey wool dress and the black jacket were not enough warmth. My teeth were chattering. I adjusted my red scarf and headphones while listening to the tune of Evanescence. I felt like I was in the My Immortal video; sad, grey, and anguished.

The bus was always late, and this was no exception. I rubbed my arms to give myself some warmth as the wait became unbearable. Anxiety was eating away at me.

When it finally arrived, I got in without even looking at the driver. I had so much on my mind… so much to say, but so little desire to talk. It wouldn't have bothered me if the bus broke down halfway and didn't take me to my destination. But today was not a day like any other, I was convinced that it was going to be the last of therapy.

Marcela always made me wait more than half an hour for my appointment, something I hated, but I knew that the day I was late, she would complain about waiting for me.

When she finally ushered me in, we again had the moment of awkward silence where she waits for me to talk and I wait for her to say something.

"How did you feel this week?"

"Good."

"Not really"

"It was routine, the same as always."

"Did you feel distressed again?"

"Yes, but I'm used to it."

I didn't want to talk; I didn't want to tell her the same old things so that she would change the subject as if what I felt didn't matter.

The pen in her right hand moved quickly over his notebook. «How much does she write?

Someday, I'm going to lose my patience and I'm going to steal her notes. It would be better if she told me what she thinks, instead of writing it down so that I never know.

"Did you work with the wheel of emotions I gave you?"

"Of course, not..."

I knew well what was happening to me and that meaningless wheel confirmed it.

"I'm sad, angry, disappointed... distraught."

I took a deep breath and pressed my forehead.

"I have been telling you what I feel for months, there is no more or less than that. I feel exactly the same as the first day I sat here."

Again, her pen moved at full speed over the paper. The silences were unbearable. I never knew if she stayed silent and stared at me because she wanted to make me think or if she didn't know what to say to me.

"What did you do this week?" Again, changing topics.

"I don't want to talk about anything else, I only think about one." I sighed loudly. "I want to talk about the emptiness in my chest that I feel from the moment I wake up until I fall asleep, if I do."

"Does talking about Ulysses' departure make you feel better?"

More meaningless questions.

"No. But how am I supposed to get over it if I don't talk about it? He left me. He left without even saying goodbye." She stopped writing and stared at me.

"When did he leave?"

"Are you seriously asking me?!"

Incredible.

Isn't she supposed to take notes to learn more about me and... remember it?

My vision began to bother me and the screaming in my ears became louder and unbearable. I rubbed my eyes and sat back on the couch. I tried to keep my right leg still, which seemed to have a life of its own. I didn't want to see her. I stared at the window. I could not believe it.

What disrespect!

"Why do you ask me the same things every time I come?"

"Your answer varies week to week. I want to know which one it is today."

"No."

I felt the anger growing inside me, like a flame that rose little by little.

"I always tell you the same thing. Ulysses left me. He's gone. He disappeared without even leaving a note, an explanation. I don't know why he did it. He left his life with me just as it was. He didn't take his clothes or anything, not even his phone. I have no way to communicate with him or find him."

"What was your relationship with him like?"

"I don't understand why every time I come it's always the same. I already answered that last week. What will the next question be? Do you know where he went?" My voice was gaining volume in a way that I didn't even know myself.

She started telling me to calm down, to try to breathe deeply, but my anger grew more and more. It was a pressure cooker ready to explode.

"Are you listening to me, Marina?"

Her pen was no longer writing. Which caused me some amusement, but not that of a joke. I pounced on her without giving her time to do anything. I snatched the pen from her hand and stuck it in her neck. She didn't even scream. She desperately grabbed her neck with both hands, but immediately became weak and could not even get up from her seat. Her blood was gushing out. She no longer moved or tried to speak. Her body remained motionless, staring at me.

I grabbed her pink notebook, now a little stained, and sat back down in my seat. I crossed my legs and started reading.

Lack of dissociation between reality and her imagination.

Moody. Temporary memory loss. Reluctance, anguish, anger.

"Memory loss? Lack of dissociation between the real and the imaginary?"

I read bewildered. Those couldn't be notes about me. I continued turning the pages and several papers fell to the floor. I looked at Marcela to check that she was still there, inert, and I bent down to grab them. I didn't know what I was seeing or reading. I saw photos of my apartment with blood stains, photos of the kitchen and bedroom. The white feather bedspread was all soaked in blood. A thousand images and intermittent memories that I did not understand passed through my mind. The last photo completely disarmed me. Ulysses lay lifeless on the bathroom floor in a pool of blood, with a kitchen knife stuck in his chest.

No! How could it be him?!

Ulysses had left months ago without leaving a trace.

He had abandoned Me!

I unfolded some pages that looked like they were photocopies and had a passport photo of me stuck in the corner. What I read seemed crazy to me. Ulysses had died from thirty-five stab wounds, one straight to the heart. My hands were shaking, I wanted to see everything as quickly as possible. I grabbed a newspaper clipping:

«... Ulises Carrasco met death at the hand of his fiancée, Marina Montez, last Saturday. ...the aggressor is admitted to a neuropsychiatric hospital... she does not seem to remember anything of what happened... »

Almost like a bucket of ice water, all the memories appeared together and crowded into my mind. I remembered the beatings, the humiliation, the heartbreaking crying. He had locked me in the bathroom after beating me almost all night. As soon as he opened the door, I pushed him and ran to the kitchen and grabbed the first thing I could to defend myself. The meat cutting knife. He hit me again in the face which knocked me to the ground and stunned me, but I didn't let go of the knife. He was determined to continue his attack; I stretched out my arm with all the strength I could and stabbed the knife into his waist. I tightened the handle and turned the blade inside, as I learned from watching Face/Off. He tried to escape by clutching his wound, but I followed him. I didn't give him any chance. I remembered every one of his mistreatments, every one of his beatings and humiliations. I stabbed him with the knife again and again, and when he finally fell on the bathroom floor, where I had been locked up all night, I gave him the last stab. I sat next to him, took a deep, almost triumphant breath, and rested for the first time in years. The ringing in my ears was getting louder. I stared at the window without thinking too much. Outside, it was starting to rain.

"Marina, are you listening to me?" Marcela was staring at me with a worried expression.

She had her notebook closed and held it tightly on her lap with the pen in her right hand. «It happened again. I no longer knew what to believe. I felt dizzy, overwhelmed, and confused.

"Y…yes."

"We'll stop it here for today." She handed me what seemed to be an exit permit.

I left the office bewildered, dazed. On the other side of the door, a man dressed in white was waiting for me to escort me to the bus that would take me back to the hospital. I got on and waited, sitting in the last seat while I focused on the raindrops hitting the bus windows. Each drop that fell was like a little piece of memory that entered my mind and completed the puzzle. Little by little, other people dressed in grey and black like me got on the bus. Some with a lost look, others angry and some with a smile that did not reach their eyes. It seems to me that, in the end, this is not going to be the last session of therapy.

Mariela Ivón Armando © 2024

GOD OF LIFE – GOD OF DEATH

The silence was broken only by the soft rustle of the breeze in the sweet, resinous scent of the firs and deep grass. The skies were a blue so rich that the pine needles were light in comparison. Distantly, the pounding roar of the waterfall reached her questing ears. She altered her course slightly, heading toward it, trusting more in her ears than her memory of landmarks. She trotted smoothly, her joints loose and relaxed under her cougar-skin smock, her bare feet thick with callus from a lifetime of travel, following the herds. Her name was Ena, named for the sound made by the mouse-deer when it was spitted on a spear. It was an insult, cast upon a newborn that would not live through the night.

But she did.

Reddish-brown, ratted tangles hung down about her muscular shoulders, the frazzled tips brushing her waist as she continued her pace, eager to catch up with the clan before sunset. Her smock was pieced together from different cougar hides, some of them the color of sand, others more red, others shaded more toward gray. All marked her as one of the Clan of the Great Cat, one of the fiercest of the clans. She was proud of her clan … even if they did hide her when fighting other clans. It would not do to have one who looked like her noticed by other clans. Her face was finely boned, with a pert nose, full lips and large, blue eyes. All were at odds with the rest of her clan, who were much heavier in the brow and nose, with dark eyes and hair. Ena favored her mother, taken captive after a battle between clans by her father. Ena was never as strong as the others were, and she did not have as keen a sense of smell, but she was faster, more nimble, and much more cunning.

Ena looked up at the sky with a gasp, then let out a relieved breath. It was only a dark mound of white drifting across the sun, not actual sunset darkening the sky. Nonetheless, it was nearer dusk than she liked. She hefted her bone-tipped spear in her left hand as she ran even harder. Not only was she further behind the others than was acceptable, she was also empty-handed, no game to show for it.

The ground steadily grew harder and less grassy as the firs closed in about her, enfolding her in dim, sweet shadow. It was welcome, helping her maintain her pace without as much of the sun's heat. Then again, it muted the sounds of Sea God's Gate, the angry waterfall that was the agreed-upon meeting place. She was no longer certain how much longer she had to run. She could just imagine coming out of the trees and stepping off the edge of the jagged cliff, to fall down with the tumbling water, just one more droplet amidst the rains of all tomorrows.

Ena burst out of the trees and stumbled to a frantic halt, not because of a deadly fall, but because of the looming monstrosity of the waterfall rising a hundred feet above. She had been wrong. She was off course, ending up at the base of the waterfall, rather than at its top. She did not understand it, but it had happened. She was in the basin, a round hole cut into the stone, and the thunder of plummeting water coming down smooth stone to a massive pool was deafening. Mist was everywhere, enshrouding its base, casting the sun's rays into the bands of the rainbow as it drifted steadily toward her. Ena smiled, letting the moisture settle on her skin and cool her overworked muscles. She extended her arms to the sides, watching droplets form on the pale hairs on her forearms, weighing them down until they slid down her skin, dragging away the dirt and leaving trails of pink behind. How could it be forbidden to enter the basin? It was wonderful.

Her spear smacked onto the bare rock at her feet as she hurriedly pulled off her single, smock-like garment. The skin crumpled in on itself in a cloud of dust, mites and burrs. Ena watched more mist condense on her skin and rubbed at it with her palms, drawing streaks of thin mud across her body. She slid both palms over her face and into her hair, exulting in the cleansing chill—

There was no pain as a bone-tipped spear tore through her flesh, parting her ribs, then meeting the rock at her feet. Dazedly, she looked down at it, jutting upward, grasped it with both hands, and looked up at the rim of the basin … where she was supposed to have met up with the rest of her clan … saw her attacker, dressed in a cougar-skin smock like the one at her feet. She tried to move, but the bone tip was caught in a crack in the stone, holding her upright until she finally fell to her side. The impact forced the breath from her lungs … and she was unable to take in another.

Death.

* * *

"So futile," the god of life said, staring into his mead-filled goblet, the last scene of Ena's life continuing to fade from its surface. His features were handsome, his jaw square and strong, his long hair black and thick, draping his broad shoulders. His skin was smooth, his frame well-muscled and powerful.

"Yes," the god of death agreed, then bit off what remained of an immortal thumbnail, and all traces of Ena winked out. He stuck out his tongue, a bit of thumbnail stuck to its pink tip, and blew sharply, dislodging it. He slid his fingertip over the uneven, partially exposed nailbed. When his thumbnail was once again exposed, it was perfect and whole. He wiped the saliva on the pale cloth draping his perfect form disinterestedly. Unlike his brother, he was thin to the point of emaciation, as if being eaten away from the inside. His black hair was thin and wispy, hanging lankly. "I cannot see why you even bother with them, Coriageddon."

The god of life drank, spilling a little down from the corner of his mouth, then looked at Dirroden over the brim of his goblet, his deep-green irises completely smooth, not even marred by pupils. He wiped the side of his mouth with the back of his wrist, spilling more mead on the uneven, stone floor of the cave. "Bother?" he repeated. "It is no bother, good brother," he breathed, sipping again from the goblet. "But it is … frustrating." He paused, then added, "At times. I had thought that, perhaps, I had found a mortal worthy of my attention."

Dirroden arched his brows and his eyes yawned wide, black sclera with perfect, white irises just as smooth and unmarred as Coriageddon's. "But you were wrong."

Coriageddon nodded, a barely perceptible movement. "Yes, good brother, I was wrong."

"Again," Dirroden said, pointing a bony finger at his brother for emphasis.

"Again," the other agreed. "Once again, you make my efforts seem futile."

Dirroden smiled. "Not futile, good brother. Your efforts do, indeed, produce."

Coriageddon drained his goblet and folded his muscular arms over his formless smock. "Very well. If not futile, then how would you describe it?"

"Foolish," the other answered quickly.

"There you are wrong, good brother," Coriageddon said, wagging a finger. "I am not devoid of good sense, nor do I lack in intellect."

"Where you are a fool, my sibling, is by showing such interest in these mortals," Dirroden stated simply. "Mortals, females in particular, are not worthy of us."

"How so?"

"We are life and death."

"I am life. Females are the fonts from which life springs." He smiled triumphantly. "They must be at least a little worthy, I would say."

Dirroden frowned at him, jaw muscles working under his paper-thin skin, then growled, "You are a fool." He bit into his thumbnail several times in succession.

Snap, snap, snap, snap!

He lifted his chin and puffed, blowing more chips negligently onto the floor.

"More lives gone," Coriageddon said, then sighed thinly. "You have bitten away more souls. Out of spite, this time." The other did not respond. Coriageddon walked slowly toward the raw, stone wall, fingertips sliding across the cave roof, leaving a trail of blue-white astral light in his wake. When he looked back, the four distinct, glowing lines remained, making his perfect form even more clear in the brighter light. "Will you ever tire of such duty? Or, at least, delay long enough for me to find even a moment's happiness?"

Dirroden frowned, then slapped the ceiling petulantly, dousing the glow with each contact as if it was a line of candle flames. When he reached Coriageddon, they stood nose to nose, the remaining focused light shining down on him. Dirroden hesitated, then turned away again, leaving what remained. "That would defeat your purpose, brother," he said. "If you found happiness, your reveries would end. Life springs forth from your fantasizing. So, no, I will never tire."

"My purpose or yours?" Coriageddon asked.

"Hmn?"

"You said my happiness would defeat my purpose. I ask if it would actually defeat yours."

Dirroden frowned at his brother, then gestured irritably. "Stop searching. Just dream, for you will never succeed." He bit another chip of nail off his thumb — snap! — and puffed it onto the stone floor between his ankles. "You will never succeed while all lives end at my feet."

Coriageddon nodded, as he had so many times before through the aeons. "Yes, good brother." He crossed the cavern of eternity, so much of it raw stone, until he reached a place where it was recessed, a space just right for him to sit and rest his arms on either side, like a great throne. He closed his eyes and reached out for a sense of comfort, and the stone warmed, exuding heat that soothed his frame. He imagined beautiful skies, green grass . . . then felt the delicate life spawned from it on Earth.

The snap of Dirroden chewing his bothersome thumbnail jerked him out of his musings, his pupil-less irises jerking toward the far side of the cave. Dirroden sat in a space just like Coriageddon's, but narrower, and they locked eyes. Coriageddon closed his eyes, exhaling softly.

Aeons are nothing for immortals, just as they are for mortals. In fact, the former might feel them more than the latter, in their thoughts, if not their physical forms. As Coriageddon considered it, he realized that mortals felt them not at all. It was an interesting concept.

As it turned out, Dirroden had been wrong. Finding happiness did not stop Coriageddon from dreaming. If anything, happiness made him dream even more. He got better at creating mortals with gifts, companions for a time, men or women. It did not matter which, because he starved for friendship other than that of his abrasive brother. He had his favorites, and even Dirroden could no longer deny him, not completely, although there was no denying mortality.

Aeons passed ....

* * *

Water, warm and burning, bore down on her, restricting her movement, cutting off her access to life-sustaining air. Her lungs burned as she struggled, arms and legs flailing more and more, her short hair swimming about her pretty face as her lips turned more blue than pink.

She had requested trial by ordeal to disprove the allegations against her. It seemed the best option after other attempts to label her a witch had failed, and her accusers were allowed to persist in their persecution. She was a good swimmer. She had swum the Great River many times over her life. What had gone wrong?

She could hear the raised voices of those on the banks, her accusers roaring that divine judgment had prevailed, while others wailed in anguish. Her muscles burned, but not as much as her lungs. She made one final thrust toward the surface and felt her face break through to open air. She opened her mouth to take a breath of air — and water poured in, down her throat and into her lungs, searing its way like liquid fire.

She was not a witch. Why was she being punished? Then the answer came. Her sin was not witchcraft, but pride. She had thought that she could use the gods to her own ends. It was no wonder that she was being punished for it, sinking down deeper and deeper, the water muting the sunlight.

Her eyelids closed before she reached the chalky bottom.

A single, small bubble rose from one nostril.

Death.

* * *

"Why do you never tire, brother?" Dirroden asked.

Coriageddon looked up from the waves of his bathing pool. The drowned woman's form faded from its ripples, and he smiled faintly. "I could ask the same of you." He slid under the warm water up to his chin, the pool cut right into the stone floor, now smooth, at the request of one of his past companions. Her name was Zahra, an Egyptian, and her remains were over to his right, with dozens of others that had been his favorites.

He sighed and slid under the surface, inhaling and exhaling, trying to imagine what it felt like to drown. He could not. He could not imagine the burning in the lungs, the inability to breathe, the panic. He simply could not. He sat up and exhaled two streams of water from his nostrils.

Dirroden waited patiently for him to finish, then said, "They think me evil, brother."

"Yes, the mortals," Coriageddon answered, more water running over his bottom lip. "The animals do not. Most of them do not see your coming. They do not anticipate your bite. Do not know it cannot be avoided."

"But the mortals know," Dirroden stated bluntly. "They give me yet another name."

Coriageddon raised his eyebrows interestedly. "A new name?" he repeated quizzically. "I am beginning to think that the more significant a thing, the more names the mortals invent for it." He hesitated, then said, "Osiris was a good name. Of course, I must admit a penchant for the Egyptians. Zahra was my first mortal companion, after all. I rather liked the name Thanatos, as well. It rolls off the tongue." He paused, then said it slowly, as if tasting the syllables. "Thanatos. I like that one. Although the tales they told of Thanatos were unflattering. The tales of Hades were much more impressive."

Snap!

Coriageddon looked sharply at Dirroden, who asked, "May I continue?"

"Of course. What is the new name, brother?"

"It comes from the word 'evil' itself," Dirroden stated expansively, an odd grin curving his lips. "Some are starting to call me Devil."

Coriageddon smiled and nodded. "How nice," he said. "Those same people have given me a new name, as well. A name derived from 'good.' They call me God."

"Do you accept this?" Dirroden asked.

Coriageddon smiled as he considered it, then nodded. "Certainly."

Dirroden frowned, pushing one of a score of mortal skulls nearer the cave wall with a negligent flick of his foot. "Of course, you do," he muttered darkly.

"My acceptance makes no difference, brother," Coriageddon said mindfully.

"But does theirs?" Dirroden asked, his voice scarcely more than a whisper, then he straightened and boomed. "They are mine, also, brother! Of your mind, but of my body!"

Coriageddon's head pulled back slightly in surprise at the rare outburst, then he climbed out of the water. "Your duty is to take of your body," he agreed. "To feel each and every death."

"It would be easier to destroy them all," Dirroden whispered. "But I do not. I control that impulse."

"Of course, you do."

"And for that, they think me evil," he growled, white irises directed at the stone floor.

"And I give of my mind, my … heart. And think that a showing of goodness."

"God, Devil," Dirroden muttered sourly.

"Good, evil," Coriageddon countered, a playful twinkle in his green, pupil-less eyes.

"Life, death," Dirroden responded, finding his own smile in return.

"Do you weary?" Coriageddon challenged quickly, finding the familiar cadence.

"No!" Dirroden snapped, clapping his bony hands, then he started to hum a gentle melody until Coriageddon joined in. Dirroden started to sing in Ancient Greek:

While you live, shine,

By no means at all, thou grieve!

For little exists, the living;

The end, the time requirest.

"Lovely," Coriageddon said, smiling.

"The mortals are the only ones who know of me," Dirroden said, his rare grin still solidly in place. "They even expect me." He raised his thumb, that bothersome nail extended past its tip almost as far as the last joint. "I should not disappoint them."

"You should not!" his brother agreed, waving his encouragement with both hands.

Snap!

Another chip of nail tumbled to the floor.

W. D. Kilpack III © 2024

OVER THE RAINBOW

at the concert   I cry
quiet tears to the tune of
somewhere over the rainbow
all that heartfelt hope   all that yearning
for a better place over there
and what do we have?

I can't wait
for the bluebirds can't wait
for the way up there

I don't know what to say
to my Jewish American friend
well intended words
rain soft but silence
rains harder
a too-long pause
across the divide a fear
of trust shattering
silence clothes wordless
anger

I hold my tongue
not knowing

José F. Nodar

where to look   for the cache
at the end of the rainbow.

105

Maree Gladwin © 2024

CORN, TURDS, COWS AND CONGRESS

I noticed all the little corn kernels in the toilet bowl when I went to flush. This wasn't the first time I've seen that, but now that I am retired, I suppose I have more time on my hands to notice things like that. If it doesn't stop, I'm gonna have to find me a job. After an hour contemplating the mystery of corn, I flushed. It left me thinking, What the hell is corn made out of where everything else you eat turns to crap, but corn comes out like new. I could probably just pick it out and put it back on your plat. I say 'your' plate, cause I'm crazy, but I'm not stupid.

Have the folks at NASA done any serious research on corn; maybe like coating the Space Shuttle with it. Seriously, if you can crap corn without messing it up, it should be able to reenter Earth's atmosphere, wouldn't you think? You can't tell me re-entry is worse than being pooped out of Uranus. You know what I'm talking about, like when you've been eating Mexican food, and it feels like a flaming meteor is passing through your 'black hole.'

The next thing you know, you've got a bad case of Asteroids. I couldn't wait on NASA, so I did my own study on corn. After an exhausted research, (after reading for ten minutes…I was exhausted), I concluded that corn is really bad stuff.

First, it seems the farmers have become addicted to corn. Not that they are smoking it, as far as I know, but they have become dependent on all the money Congress gives them for growing corn. Some of the corn they give to their cows. This has caused the cows to become addicted—not that they are smoking it either, as far as I know.

The cows have become dependent on all the drugs they have to take because they eat the corn. When the cows eat the corn, they get a stomach ache because the corn allows E. Coli and His Gang of Misfits, which are bacteria or a heavy metal band, to thrive in the cows stomach which is a bad thing. For those of you who aren't up on bovine 'anata-moo-me,' cows have three stomachs which means they have to have a triple dose of drugs. That is why they eat so much corn so they can keep getting the drugs.

Originally, cows were perfectly healthy and contented with grass, even if they were a bit paranoid. Then the Government got involved—the next thing you know cows were doing hard drugs with needles. That led to planes from Columbia landing in the pastures late at night to deliver drugs directly to the bovines, bypassing the middleman.

Having a beef with lengthy deliveries caused the heifers to hoof it down to the city to meet with a dealer to get a fix. It wasn't long after that the public witnessed rival herds of cattle like the Holsteins and the Herefords, already wearing 'leather' jackets but now branded with their gang's logo, stampeding on each other's turf.

Bulls began pimping the females in the herd to get money for drugs and guns. Between the FBI, DEA, and ASPCA, there aren't going to be any more hamburgers. Then, when someone asks, 'Where's the Beef,' the answer will be that all the cows are serving time at the…state…pen… for possession, distribution, cattle trafficking, and racketeering.

Congressmen are very high on corn. They are not smoking it, as far as I know, but they keep giving large subsidies to the farmers to keep growing corn. They like all the money that corporations give to those who need huge quantities of corn to make their products.

One figure said that of the 10,000 items in a grocery store, 2,500 of them were made with corn, and that is just the beginning. They are putting corn products in stuff like tires and make-up, building materials, and even explosives. Darn! You better be careful or maybe the corn will blow out your o-ring. Supposedly, it is the corn products in our food that are making us fat, upsetting world trade, and using up all the land to grow more corn.

Corn has also been blamed for global hunger, global warming (from all the cow farts in the ozone layer), impotence (I need to blame that on something), and Irritable Bowel Syndrome. I don't know how they came up with 'irritable' in IBS because if I had pain and cramps with diarrhea and constipation, they'd have to change the name to 'Grumpy SOB Bowel Syndrome.' I'm not a medical doctor, though I have pretended to be a gynecologist, but that is another story.

If our bodies use the food it needs for fuel and discard the remainder either by (medically speaking) pooping, peeing or farting, it would seem that our bodies have no use for corn. It should also be important to note that any interruption in the aforementioned pooping, peeing, or farting could result in death. I don't know about you, but I wouldn't want anyone at my funeral saying, "He lived like he died, full of…it."

Speaking of which, I'm reading up on folks eating corn and you know how they say you can be given too much information? Well, here is a perfect example. I really don't know who said this, but I seriously doubt they'd admit it. If a family wanted to learn more about their digestive systems, they could do an interesting experiment at home. The basic idea is for Dad, Mom, Brother, and Sis to each consume half a can of Corn Nibblets. Then gather together as each member of the family craps them out.

While I've read about families on the Internet doing some really kinky perverted stuff that would be illegal every where in the world except West Virginia and parts of Kentucky. This is probably legal there has got to be something dysfunctional about this family when dad yells, "Hey everybody," come quick before I flush, and see the corn in my turds."

"Wow Father, you must have been full of crap!" Suzie said without thinking.

"Oh Honey, wheeew," his wife exclaimed, holding her nose. "You promised me you'd lay off the tacos."

"Gee, that's nothing Dad," exclaimed Billy, "wait until you see what I crapped. Let's just hope the bag don't break or we're all dead!" The family also did variations on what they eat and see how that speeds up or slows down their bowel movements using the corn as a marker. What kind of twisted, brain-dead, weird-o family would be chugging down corn on a Friday night so they can gather around the bowl on Sunday for turd comparison and meditation. What I do know is that if one word of this gets out you can damn well figure on seeing a new show with contestants doing this on FOX next season. Sort of like the 'Great Race,' where contestants would compete to see who's colon was faster, to win exciting prizes.

You could say I am being ridiculous…I would ask, 'Have you ever seen Fear Factor.' However, on this show you would have to have a judge to examine the evidence with a stop watch. I am positive it would at least be as popular as 'Lost,' 'Survivors,' and other crap like the 'View' phew! The only difference is that the 'View' only features five 'butt holes, not counting a guest.

Why then do we even eat corn at all? Scientifically speaking, one theory would be that it sure tastes great with some butter and a little salt. Another possibility would be that it makes our turds look interesting. For me, it gave me something to write about as I pissed away another day of retirement down here in Florida.

Grizzly G. Gus © 2024

QUESTIONS

Sometimes, there are questions we don't ask. It's not that we don't want to ask, or that we're afraid of hearing the answer, but rather because some subjects are difficult to raise in everyday conversation. In my case it was partly the above, but also because I chose not to think about it.

Leigh was always economical with words. So much of our time together was spent in silence—each of us immersed in an engrossing task of some kind, whether it be a novel, a textbook, a movie, Leigh's quilting, or the evening paper. Never much of a talker myself, I found this part of our relationship strangely fulfilling, as if there was little need for platitudes or empty conversation. We always kept one promise though: we never ended the day without saying 'I love you'.

Now, when I visit her each day, I still utter those words before leaving, even though I've no guarantee she hears them. Sometimes she's awake when I call; sometimes she sleeps. Either way, she doesn't acknowledge my presence. One of the nursing staff told me the other day that she heard Leigh say my name after I'd left. Maybe she did; maybe she didn't. I only know that since her fall and subsequent stroke, my Leigh has been conspicuous by her absence. A hollow facsimile of the woman I knew and loved.

Seven years is a long time. In the bigger overall picture, though, it's also a very short time—less than ten percent of my life so far, in fact. When I think back now over all the things we've shared during those seven years, it seems simultaneously both an aeon and a heartbeat.

Illness and impending death are no strangers to either of us. Our marriage is a case of third time lucky for us both. We each married young—some would say in haste. We raised children who would later turn their backs on us and suffered through bitter divorces. Our second marriages were happier, but short-lived. Each of our spouses suffered debilitating illness; illness that necessitated constant care before they finally left us—alone once more. This shared history was, I believe, the catalyst that fired the cosmic and chemical reaction that brought and held us together. Now, even that is dissipating.

Sitting in the arbour outside her window, I contemplate the questions we didn't ask. If I were a smoker, as in my younger days, I'd probably have gone through an entire packet today without even noticing. Instead, I sit and stare into the distance and try to imagine what Leigh's answers might have been.

Given our circumstances, you'd think we might have been more open to the discussion; more comfortable maybe, but we each chose the same path. With no proper agreement or debate, we each chose the path of silence.

"Starting to turn a bit chilly, isn't it?" I glance in the direction of the voice. A young nurse, possibly the same one who fetched me a cup of tea earlier, is enjoying a cigarette out of sight of the lunchroom.

"Yeah," I reply. "Autumn's nearly over. Now comes the Winter of our Discontent."

I poke at a discarded cigarette butt with one toe. She doesn't reply. Probably trying to decide if she's actually heard that phrase before, and if so—where.

"Richard the Third," I explain. "Act one, Scene one, though I'm paraphrasing."

"Shakespeare?" She furrows her brow. "Oh. I thought it was… oh, never mind." She shrugs.

"Never doubt the uselessness of a college education." I toss this pearl of wisdom as much to myself as to her.

"You're Leigh's, er …"

"Partner," I offer. "I believe that's the appropriate term these days. We never bothered about marriage. Both been through that before, more than once. Didn't either of us see the need to do it again."

She takes another long drag before blowing a cloud of toxic smoke skyward. "How long …" Her voice trails off. "Sorry, it's none of my business. I'm a nosy bitch sometimes. I'm always getting told off for asking personal questions."

She quickly leans in toward me.

"You won't say anything about it, will you—please? It's just that I'm on a warning about getting too close to patients and their families."

"Relax, Girlie," I say. "I appreciate the fact that you're interested enough to ask. Most couldn't care less and aren't afraid to show it." Another question goes unanswered.

After a moment's silence, she speaks again. "Julie. My name—it's Julie."

"Hello, Julie. Good to know you."

We sit in collective silence for several minutes, during which she finishes her smoke and grinds the stub beneath one sensible work shoe.

"I'm off in an hour," she says casually. "Can I buy you a coffee?"

I consider my reply. "Well, I can only assume that someone such as yourself would definitely not be hitting on me, so yes, thanks, Julie. I reckon I'd like that."

She places both hands over her mouth, blushing deeply. "Oh, shit. No. I … I mean, no, nothing like that. You just look so … like you need someone to talk to, I guess."

I laugh aloud—possibly for the first time in months. Her discomfort is palpable.

"Relax, Gir … er, Julie. I'm pulling your leg."

Rising to my feet, I offer her my hand. "Brian. Call me Brian. I'm about to go for a long walk—there's something I have to contemplate. Meet you back here at …" I consult my watch, "five?"

"Sure, see you then." She walks briskly away, leaving me to my solitude once more.

I admire her retreating figure, and I'm struck by how much she reminds me of my eldest daughter when I last saw her. Val would have been about her age now, had she lived—and assuming my estimate of Julie's age is accurate. Chuckling at her chagrin, I make my way off in the direction of a nearby park.

I return at seven minutes before the hour, still no closer to the answers I need.

She emerges at five past: smiling, confident, well-groomed. Her hair, no longer constrained in a tight ballerina bun, cascades over her shoulders, challenging the beauty of the diminishing sunshine. "Val!" I almost say. Instead, I offer her my arm, and she slips her hand in at my elbow.

"Did you come to a decision, then?" Julie says as we promenade across the grass.

"You hinted at something you had to think about," she adds in response to my puzzled look.

"Oh. No, not really." We allow the silence to hang between us as we walk.

"So how come a pretty thing like yourself is spending time with an old fart like me?" I ask. "Boyfriend let you down?"

"There's no-one at the moment," she says. "I have a flatmate, but he's gay, so I guess he doesn't count.

"I was engaged," she adds after another pause, "but he had a fling with my best friend."

"So, you lost a fiancé and a best friend."

She nods.

"Can I help? You know, with the thing you have to make a decision about?"

"I'm really not sure if anyone can help," I reply. "Are you a good listener, though?"

"The best," she says, polishing her fingernails on her cardigan and pretending to admire her reflection in them, just the way Val used to.

* * *

"Cappuccino?" I ask, pulling out a chair for her. The café is almost empty. Thirty minutes before closing time.

"I'm supposed to be treating you," she says.

"Don't worry, I'll let you pay," I push her chair in and wave a waitress over before seating myself opposite her.

"How long have you worked at the hospital?"

"Almost three years."

I hesitate, wondering whether to ask the next question.

"You're going to ask me about patients who die, aren't you." A statement, not a question.

"Have you seen many patients die?"

"A few. Most of those in our care pass in their sleep."

"Do you suppose they …"

"If you're asking if I believe in an afterlife, the answer's yes."

We're still staring into each other's eyes—mine cataract-grey, tired; hers bright, and as blue as the ocean—when our drinks arrive. How does she seem to know what I'm thinking? Another question destined never to be asked.

"You seem so sure, Val."

"Julie," she corrects me.

"Oh. Of course. Sorry, you remind me of someone, that's all."

"She's aware that you're there. You know that, don't you?"

"I like to think she is. It's so hard to be sure, though."

"Trust me, she knows."

She sips her coffee delicately, watching for my response.

"I've come to accept that she won't be with us much longer." I say.

"There are so many things I wish we'd talked about. So many questions I wish I'd asked."

"You can still ask them," Julie says. "Just because she can't speak doesn't mean she won't answer you."

"Actually," I say after a pause, "there's only one question, really. Everything else is just window-dressing."

"So, ask her," she whispers, placing a hand on mine. "You might be surprised."

The rest of our 'date' passes quickly and I'm soon walking back to where my car sits waiting in the hospital carpark. I sneak into the ward and sit at Leigh's bedside.

I take her hand as firmly as I dare and whisper, "Can you hear me? Do you really know I'm here?" I feel her pulse, but nothing more.

"You won't believe what happened. A gorgeous young nurse hit on me and shouted me a cappuccino," I gloat, before adding, "Yeah, well maybe that's not exactly true, but she did buy me a coffee."

Still no response. I lean closer, placing my lips against Leigh's ear. "There's something I have to ask. Please, if you hear me, let me know."

Her rhythmic breathing, assisted by the ventilator, is barely audible. Her hand twitches ever so slightly. Did I imagine that? I decide it was simply an involuntary spasm.

Softly, I ask my question, whispering it into her ear as she sleeps— Perchance to dream?

After several minutes I make my departure, detouring for a take-away pizza before heading home.

* * *

The phone wakes me just after 4 am. The news I've been dreading yet anticipating: Leigh was pronounced dead fifteen minutes ago. No, there's no need to come in now. Yes, please see the reception desk first thing in the morning. I flop onto the settee and switch on the television in a vain attempt to fill the void and allow the tears to flow.

Ten o'clock finds me at the reception desk, where one of the nurses hands me a scribbled note. "Sister Jenkins says Leigh woke briefly last night, around one am."

I look at the scrawl. 'Albany—Frenchman', it reads. "Does this make sense to you?" she asks, furrowing her brow.

"Perfect sense," I reply. "Thank you."

Albany Western Australia: Where we'd spent our last holiday. Where Leigh had said, "I could spend eternity looking at this view," as we admired the vista overlooking Frenchman Bay from the Marine Drive lookout. Where one day soon I would scatter Leigh's ashes; a westerly wind at my back and a tear in my eye.

"Oh, will you give a message to Julie from me?" I ask.

"Julie?"

"Yes. The pretty nurse with the honey-blonde hair. About yay tall." I indicate a height level with my earlobes.

She purses her lips, shaking her head slightly. "No nurse here named Julie," she says. "Are you sure you've got the name right?"

"I thought I had, but maybe it was Valerie," I reply.

She's shaking her head again, so I simply say, "No matter. I think she knows."

Thomas Greenbank © 2024

THE PORTAL

His mother's words rained down like a thunderstorm.

"You're in the way, Bao. I almost fell on you!"

The small boy, no more than sixty pounds, stumbled to a stop, cringing as his knees buckled. With all his might, he stood up straight and struggled to hold the heavy tub of coconut oil. He needed to carry it across the slippery kitchen floor and dropping it would be a disaster. He wanted help. He wanted to complain to her, but he knew he would only receive a sharp lecture, if she responded at all. Wishing he could disappear into the hot steamy mist, he staggered to a spot near the wall.

"I'll go around you!" she grumbled.

He tightened his little arms around his greasy burden and held it tight against his chest. Drops of sweat stung his eyes and he did his best to blink them away. He looked up at his mother in the dim light but could not see her face through the armload of bok choy she carried.

He heard her drop the white vegetables on a high wooden counter and knew he could move again. He adjusted the tub and resumed walking toward the huge iron stove that was the heart of the Nhà Rộng (Big House) restaurant.

Thick steam filled the kitchen as orange flames licked up from the stovetop. Bao could just make out the silhouette of his father standing alongside two other cooks. All three men busily stirred vegetables, shrimp, and pork in their sizzling woks. He walked carefully toward them. No windows brightened the kitchen. Only a screen door opened to the alley outside. It provided faint light and did nothing to vent the stifling heat.

Bao reached his father and nudged the tub against the man's leg. Quan turned and looked down at his eldest son. "Give it to me," he said. Bao strained to lift the tub higher, but only raised it a few inches. "I'll get it," his father said as he reached down and swept it from Bao's arms. The sudden lightness made Bao feel like he might float away. He watched his father place the tub on a shelf next to the stove and resume cooking.

He turned and encountered his mother again.

"Take this out," she commanded, handing him a dark green, lumpy trash bag nearly as large as he was. Grasping its neck with both hands, he dragged it across the floor to the exit.

Outside, the screen door closed behind him, and he set the bag down on the narrow landing. He stopped there and wiped his forehead with the back of his hand. Before him, two steps led down to an alley between the restaurant and the laundromat next door. He glanced to his left where the alley dead-ended at a brick wall some thirty feet away. Turning back, he looked across the way at a windowless wall that held a single closed door. He stared at it for a moment before hauling the bag down to the ground and over to the huge dumpster on his right.

A flimsy wooden crate stood alongside the blue metal behemoth, and he climbed onto it. Wrinkling his nose at the odor of rotting trash, he pressed the bag against the side of the dumpster and, pushing up from the bottom, shoved it up and over the top. It landed inside with a soft thump, and his arms collapsed at his sides.

Despite the rancid smell, he remained standing there. A little Vietnamese boy, nearly eight years old, he listened for a moment to the traffic on Manhattan's Ninth Avenue. Then he stepped down, but instead of returning to the kitchen, he walked deeper into the alley, toward the brick wall at the far end. He felt daring and excited, full of bravado. *I can walk away if I want to!*

As he neared the wall, he thought he might rest against it for a moment. But a wisp of wind grazed his face, and he entered another world. The air was different, warm and clean, so unlike the soured alley. Rich dark earth felt soft under his sneakers. A curtain of green leaves hung before him in a multitude of shades and shapes and sizes. There were large dark ones as big as a wok and others that were pale green, looking soft and glimmering in the mottled light. They waved to him, and he pushed his little hands ahead to part them.

He stepped through the opening he had made and found he was in a clearing. At the far side, he saw big ferns and tall plants with bright yellow, pink, and blue flowers. The world around him had transformed into a lush tropical oasis. He stood still, taking in the dazzling colors, delighting in this sparkling, wondrous new place. For the first time in a long time, he felt happy and free. He knew he couldn't stay long, but for this brief moment, he could experience beauty and serenity, away from the stifling kitchen.

Then his calm was shattered by a deafening roar that pierced his ears and sent him stumbling backward. He turned and ran through the trees and out of the clearing.

He was back in the alley, and he looked around, trying to understand what had happened. Was it a dream? He didn't think so. There was no explanation, and he ran back to the kitchen.

As soon as he was inside, his mother grabbed him and shook his bony shoulders. "Where have you been?" she shouted. "I looked everywhere for you." She let go of him and picked up a bamboo cane she kept on a shelf. She smacked him with it on his side and yelled, "Over two hours!"

He held up a small hand, trying to defend himself. "No! I went outside, just for a second."

"A second!" she snorted. "Don't do that again. You stay here!'

He shivered and looked back toward the screen door. The sky had darkened. It was much later than he expected, and the kitchen was bustling now, well into the dinner hour. "I'm sorry," he mumbled. That was a dream, he told himself sharply. I fell asleep and had a dream. It wasn't real.

* * *

One week later, on a late September afternoon when no one was after him to do something, he walked to the screen door and looked out at the alley. Glancing quickly behind him and hoping no one saw him go, he slipped out and stood again at the top of the steps.

He stared blankly across the way, with no particular plan, when a heavyset young woman with long black hair emerged from the door of the laundromat. Normally, that door remained closed, and it surprised him to see anyone come through it.

The woman glanced at him and then turned and strode away to his left, toward the back of the alley. As she neared the brick wall, she vanished. He squinted at the spot where she had been. Where did she go? There was nowhere she could go. She had completely disappeared. He tried to think. Is she with the dinosaurs? Is she a ghost? Another dream?

Throughout his life, Bao had heard chuyện ma, ghost stories. People who died unhappy deaths became ghosts. She must have been a ghost, maybe a bad one. He waited a moment longer, and when she did not reappear, he turned and dashed back into the kitchen.

He found his mother at the vegetable counter just inside the door. Anh was busily slicing a cabbage, and he tugged at her shirt. "Come see! A woman in the alley. A ghost! She disappeared!" He tried to pull her to the door.

"What?" she asked, shaking him off and continuing to cut the cabbage. She did not look at him. "What?" she asked again.

He stared up at her and spread his hands out from his sides. "A ghost. I saw her. She came into the alley and now she's gone." He stood on his toes, waiting for a response, but she still did not look his way.

At last, his mother stopped what she was doing and looked down at him. His eyes were wide open and he was trembling slightly. With a shake of her head, she handed him a large plastic trash bag. "Here, hold this," she said. "Hold it open."

Bao clenched his teeth, but did as he was told, and she dumped into the bag onion skins, bok choy leaves, loose bean sprouts, and other kitchen scraps.

He tried one more time. "She disappeared! I think she was a ghost!" But his mother said nothing and resumed slicing the cabbage. With a tightly closed mouth, he shoved the bag against the wall next to her and retreated to a corner of the room.

* * *

At 9:00 p.m. that night, in the Queens apartment that Bao's family shared with two older cousins, Bao knelt down on the floor next to a lumpy mattress. His five-year-old brother Binh was already asleep, facing the wall. Making space for himself, Bao slid his plastic dinosaur collection off his side of the bed and lay down, but he dared not shut his eyes. He had seen a ghost and he worried it would come back and take him while he slept. With his little brother breathing peacefully beside him, Bao remained awake for many hours before finally falling into a fitful sleep just before dawn.

As the sun rose and light crept in through the pale curtains, everyone else was awake, dressing, heating pho for breakfast, and talking among themselves, but Bao remained asleep.

His mother reached down and gently squeezed his shoulder. "You must get up, Bao. Time for school."

The boy looked up at her, blinking his eyes. "What?" he asked, not fully awake. He knew he had been angry with her but could not recall why.

"Happy birthday," she said. She kissed the top of his head and squeezed his shoulder again. "Up now," she smiled. He did not move. "Why are you so sleepy?" she asked.

He wiped his eyes and remembered. "At work, in the alley, there's a ghost. Maybe here too," he added anxiously.

She peered at him for a moment and shook her head. "Get dressed now."

He rose slowly, put on his clothes, and said nothing more.

In his second-grade class that day, Bao fell asleep at his desk, earning him a sharp rebuke from Mrs. Robinson, his teacher. Later in the afternoon, back at the restaurant, he found himself standing near the stove, not sure how he had gotten there. In his drowsy state, he nearly stumbled into it, causing a cook to push him away and scold him for being underfoot.

All day he avoided going into the alley or even looking outside, but just before leaving that evening, he stole one furtive glance out the screen door and then quickly turned away.

* * *

That night, his mother celebrated his birthday in the American way. Bao, his father, and Binh sat around their little kitchen table as Anh stood behind her older boy. She placed before him a small cake crowded with eight flickering candles and whispered in his ear that he should blow out them out and make a wish. Bao struggled to think of one as the candles burned down.

"Hurry," his mother urged.

He decided to wish that the ghost would go away, and he announced that wish out loud. Everyone, even Binh, laughed at that. Shaking her head a little, his mother leaned over his shoulder and cut a small piece of cake for him. "Happy birthday," she said.

Although pleased by her attention, Bao only took a small bite and stared silently at the table.

* * *

After a week of restless nights and sleep-deprived days, Bao summoned the courage to investigate the alley. She's a good ghost, he insisted to himself. In the fading afternoon light, he pushed cautiously through the screen door and walked down the steps. Nobody saw him leave, but a dishwasher from the restaurant stood outside in the alley smoking a cigarette. Bao started toward the man, who shook his head, turned, and walked farther down the alley. Bao decided the man wanted to be left alone, so he climbed back up the steps and watched from there.

As the man neared the far wall, he vanished. It happened again. He disappeared! He must be another ghost! Bao ran inside and tried to tell his mother, but she would not listen. Instead she pointed to a mop and bucket in a corner. "Mop this floor," she ordered.

When the dishwasher had not come back that night or the next day, Mr. Trong, Bao's uncle and the owner of Nhà Rộng, told everyone the man had decided not to return to work. But Bao knew differently. Although he rarely spoke to his rich uncle, who lived in his own big house, Bao tried to explain. "He turned into a ghost."

Uncle Trong looked down at him as if he were considering the possibility. "No, he just went away. He's somewhere else now."

Bao nodded gravely. He believed the dishwasher had joined the other ghost.

* * *

At home a few nights later, Anh sat at the kitchen table and opened a letter from Mrs. Robinson. She carefully read the teacher's words. Bao's performance had declined drastically. He was sleeping in class, telling wild stories, disrupting the other children, and his schoolwork was suffering. The teacher suggested maybe Bao was working too many hours at the family restaurant.

Anh threw down the letter, stood up, and found her son. "Bao, work harder in school," she shouted. "What's the matter with you!"

Bao attempted to explain yet again about the ghosts and the disappearing people, but his mother had no patience with him. "Stop telling stories!" she yelled. "You must do better." Bao sputtered in protest, but she pinched his upper arm. He whimpered at the pain and burst into tears. She looked down at him, her eyes fiery with rage. "You must work harder! Now go to bed."

Bao wiped the tears from his cheeks with his small fists and ran to his mattress.

The next morning, he sorted through his dinosaur collection until he found the little plastic Triceratops. Thinking it looked fierce and strong, he put it in his pants pocket.

That afternoon his mother was working in the front of the restaurant, and Bao saw an opportunity to slip away. No one saw him leave the kitchen and walk out the door and into the alley. One step from the wall, he hesitated, fearing the ghosts beyond, but then he sensed a breeze and the sweet smell of rich plant life, and he stepped through the portal.

As before, moist air warmed his arms. Again, he faced a curtain of large tropical leaves swaying in the wind, and he pushed through these. He was back in the clearing. A wide grin filled his face. Across the way, he saw the leafy plants, big ferns, and bright flowers. He loved it here, and he rushed across the grass, avoiding some rocks and muddy spots. At the other side he stopped, panting with excitement, and felt a shiver of expectation shoot through his chest. He took a deep breath.

Standing before the second leafy curtain, he heard faint whooshing sounds and snorting grunts. He pushed the branches and leaves aside and poked his head through. A vast lake glowed in the sun, and gigantic, long-necked dinosaurs stood in the shallow water, chewing on waving grasses. Bao craned his neck, trying to see everything in the wide watery landscape. He felt the little Triceratops in his pocket and thought this time when I come back, I will bring a dinosaur with me. He was determined to lead a dinosaur back and send it rampaging through Nhà Rộng.

Then something touched his shoulder from behind, and he whirled around. The dishwasher, who had vanished days before, waved at him with one hand and gripped his upper arm with the other. He pulled Bao back into the clearing.

Bao wrenched his arm free, but he tripped and fell face down in the grass and dirt, muddying his shirt and scraping his knee on a sharp rock. He staggered back to his feet and brushed some of the dirt off his chest. The dishwasher grabbed his arm again, tighter this time.

"Let me go!" Bao said, trying to wriggle away.

"Quiet!" the dishwasher hissed and pulled Bao back to the other side of the clearing. The man looked around fearfully. "We can talk here," he said.

Bao stared up at his captor, studying him. "You're not a ghost?"

"No." The dishwasher shook his head. "We must go back now. It is dangerous here. Do you know the way?"

"I want to get a dinosaur."

"You're crazy. I saw a lady get hurt. We have to leave now."

Bao tried to remain planted where he was. He had only been there ten minutes or so, and he wished to explore further. "I don't want to go back yet," he said. "I want to stay here," but the man held his arm, clearly afraid to be in this place another moment.

Bao had no choice. This grown man towed him along the edge of the clearing. Finally, they came to a stop. The dishwasher flailed with his free hand. "Where? Where?" he demanded.

Bao knew exactly where he had entered, and he pointed hesitantly to a spot a few yards ahead. He hated to leave without a dinosaur, but the man pulled him hard, dragging him to the stand of trees Bao had indicated.

If I stay here, Má will worry I'm not back, Bao thought. I can come back later. He reached with his free hand and showed the dishwasher the opening through which he had come.

Still clutching Bao's arm tightly, the man rushed through, pulling the boy after him. A moment later, they were back in the alley, and Bao sniffed the familiar sour smell. He looked back to the wall behind him, but the man yanked him toward the kitchen. "Come!" he insisted.

With Bao stumbling behind him, the dishwasher pulled the boy up the steps to the door and entered the kitchen. Bao noticed his mother was not at the counter to his left. He decided she was still out front and he thought she would not know he had been gone fifteen minutes.

At the stove, Quan noticed a slight shift in the air as the door behind him opened. He stopped stirring vegetables and turned, hoping his son might have come through the door. Instead, he saw the missing dishwasher. But a moment later, he spied Bao behind the man. His son was dressed in a dirty shirt and torn pants, with one knee exposed.

Quan dropped his chuan, his spatula, and ran across the kitchen. He reached around the dishwasher and lifted up his boy, hugging him tightly. "Oh, oh Bao," he shouted, "We were so worried. We could not find you. Where have you been? You were gone so long!" He looked angrily at the dishwasher. "Were you with this man all this time?"

In his father's arms, Bao felt like he was being crushed, but he had never felt so loved. "It wasn't so long," he said.

"It has been over two weeks! Your mother and I, your cousins, your brother; we were all so worried. And now you are here. I must call your mother." He put Bao down and hurried to the wall phone in the narrow hallway between the kitchen and the restaurant.

Ahn was home staring at the street through their kitchen window. She jumped up to answer the ringing phone and heard her husband shout, "He's here!"

"Bring him home now!" she yelled back.

Saying nothing to the dishwasher or his fellow cooks, Quan pulled his son through the restaurant and out the front door. "We're going home."

Bao thought it was too early to leave work. "Why?" he asked, his little feet rushing to keep up with his father.

Out on the sidewalk, Quan looked down at his boy and shook his head. "You've been gone for two weeks, even more. We thought we would never see you again! Your mother has been very upset. The police, everyone, looked for you. We thought you were lost. Come now."

"Two weeks?" Bao asked. It seemed like fifteen minutes.

They walked to the corner bus stop where Quan paused and squatted down, eye-to-eye with his boy. "Where were you all this time?"

Bao thought for a moment as cars, trucks, and buses roared down the avenue. Horns honked and brakes squealed. A herd of dinosaurs swirled through his mind, and he put a hand in his pocket and squeezed his tiny Triceratops. No one believed me before. He will not believe me now. He shook his head and stared at the sidewalk. "I don't know," he said.

Quan placed his hands on his son's shoulders. "You scared us very much, all of us. We love you. Please don't run away again." He paused and studied Bao's downcast eyes. "You weren't with that man?"

Bao shook his head.

"Was it because you were working too much at the restaurant?"

Bao looked into his father's dark eyes. "Yes," he whispered.

"So you ran away. Why didn't you tell us? You should have said something."

Bao's throat tightened up, his mouth dry. His tongue felt thick and he could not speak for a moment. But then he squeezed the dinosaur in his pocket again and said softly, "I wanted to." It was more than that, he thought, more than the restaurant. He went on, "I tried to. Nobody would listen to me."

Quan squeezed his boy's shoulders and nodded. "We will change that."

Paul Backalenick © 2024

THE SADNESS THAT HITS SO DEEP

There's a sadness that hit so quick

It came about in blindness

A grief interwoven into the threads of all

That's made me - me

Another soul taken - far before ever one should be

And madness ensues with the dismissive wave

Of those in authority.

Congregating, as we are - why do so many fail to see

The urge for truth - boiling, like a rage unsilenced inside me?

Cries from within dare to perk up

Demanding answers for what has been done

And still it seems that those forces remain unanswered - as if they're goading,

Like they've won.

As long as I breathe, I'll challenge these fiends

And never will I just remain quiet.

Some of us were born to do more than just exist -

we were brought here to try it

To try to challenge this evil force

And stand up with courage in the face of distress

And fight for truth to set us all free

Til the end of the end -

As we all deserve to be.

Sai Marie Johnson © 2024

THE LAST CALL

The sound of the tires on the gravel was stunning me. The road was rough and made us shake in the car. Nicolás, the Uber driver, was driving slowly due to the state of the road. She could see his suffering face in the rearview mirror every time he grabbed a pit.

I rubbed my hands nervously. I didn't like being so far from the city. To distract myself, I focused on what I could see out the window. We made our way through leafy trees and lots of vegetation. Very occasionally, I could see an old building, but it didn't seem like a place where many people lived. It wasn't a place I liked. The humidity, the suffocating heat, and the mosquitoes could already be felt from inside the car.

"We are almost there."

Hearing that statement made me a little more nervous, but I was glad we didn't have to go further into the forest.

We started to shake a little more when we reached a dirt road and some mud from the morning rain. I felt a louder noise and shake that threw me to the other side of the back seat. Nicolás began to brake and try to maintain control of the car that was moving from one side to the other.

"Careful!" I managed to say but it was too late.

We lurched forward as the Volkswagen's hit one of the trees to the right. I remained half hugging the front seat with my heart beating at such a speed that I felt like it was going to come out of my body. Nicolás turned around to see how I was doing. At that moment, I saw that he had a cut on his forehead and blood was falling over his right eye.

"Are you OK?" I asked in a low voice. "You're bleeding."

"Yeah. It's no big deal. You got hurt?"

I shook my head, and we got out to see how damaged the car was. The car, which was previously impeccable, had now been compacted like an accordion, a tire was completely burst, and a little smoke was coming out of the hood. I realized that I was not going to reach my destination as I had planned.

On foot and with my bags on my back, I continued walking until I reached a path that led to my great-aunt's house.

When did I last see her? I don't even remember it; perhaps years before her confinement in this place, so unsuitable for someone who is 83. Margarita, Marga, as she wanted to be called, has always been a good but lonely woman. She had no children or immediate family; She only had me left. Leaving everything and traveling almost five hundred miles to come help her was not the best plan I had, but I felt that I owed it to her for everything she had taught me as a child: to embroider, to sew, to be respectful and to behave.

I compared the image in front of me to the one on Google Maps on my phone. I had arrived at my destination, a house that was covered by vines; I imagined that it wouldn't look better inside. I left everything on the porch, even my sneakers, which were covered in mud. My legs were splashed up to my knees.

I knocked on the door, but no one answered. I knocked again, and it opened on its own accompanied by a squeak.

"Hello Marga, I arrived." I didn't want to scare her.

I entered slowly, and the smell made me close my eyes and cover my mouth. The fog didn't let me breathe. I went inside and opened every window in my path. The house was dark, with the walls covered in old, peeling wallpaper. The dusty picture frames did not allow their contents to be clearly seen. Suddenly, I felt trapped, I was out of breath. I ran back to the porch.

"It's okay, breathe." I repeated to myself, almost in a whisper.

I took a breath and went back inside. I called her again and louder. I entered through an almost endless hallway that led to the kitchen. I began to fear the worst. I retraced my steps and started searching the rooms. I opened a door but there were only boxes in the dark. The window was boarded up, I couldn't imagine why. I opened another door, the tartar on the taps, on the bidet and the nauseating smell made me so sick that I closed it instantly. There were only two more doors. One of them opened onto a room with a small bed and a dresser. Marga was not there. I headed to the last door but couldn't open it. I tried but it seemed stuck.

"Don't open it!" I jumped when I heard her dry voice behind me.

Marga was no longer who I remembered. She had white, flowing hair and her face was drawn and very pale. The white and light blue nightgown was too old for someone who usually wore fine clothes. Her hard, wrinkled look filled me with different feelings. How could someone who had everything end up like this?

"What are you doing here?" I was surprised by her abruptness; didn't she recognize me?

"Marga… I'm Sabrina."

"I know."

"I came because you called me the day before yesterday, on Saturday at noon, and you said you needed to see me. Don't you remember? I heard you very badly, and that's why I came as quickly as I could."

She looked at me thoughtful and serious.

"Now is not a good time."

She staggered and looked like she was going to fall, so I walked over and grabbed her arm. When I touched her, a chill ran through my body. She was freezing.

"Let's go to the kitchen to sit down."

She didn't respond but allowed herself to be helped. I was very quiet, I looked around and everything looked dirty. There were unwashed dishes with old food.

I tried to distract her and told her how I had arrived and why I was barefoot and dirty, but she didn't seem to pay attention to me. She stared down the hallway toward the entrance of the house.

What happened to the kind and loving woman I knew? How distressing it was to see her like that! What could I do to help her? The smell of the house, the way she looked and the way she treated me were unusual for her. I didn't want to pressure her, but if she called me after so long it was because she really needed help. I looked at her trying to see if she was beaten or sick, but her face didn't show any of that.

She got up and began to walk, shuffling her feet and clicking her slippers down the hallway. She was holding on to the walls, so I didn't think too much about it and went to help her walk.

"Let me help you."

She didn't speak to me, but she allowed me to accompany her. Two steps later, she started coughing and gagging, so I carried her to the bathroom. I went in with her thinking about breathing as little as possible due to the smell. We stood in front of her sink, and I wet her face and her hair a little, combing her hair back. We looked at each other through the mirror and she smiled at me for the first time that day.

"Thank you," I heard almost in a whisper.

I was overcome with grief, rubbed her arms affectionately, and told her she'd better go to bed.

We left the bathroom, and I took her to the bedroom, half hugging her to help her walk.

Every time I saw her more livid. Instead of entering the first door past the bathroom, she made me continue to the next one, the one I hadn't been able to open before. She touched the handle and opened it easily. We entered, and I felt next to the threshold in search of the light key. I found it on the third try.

The room lit up and my heart instantly stopped. I looked at her in despair. Her body, which I had been holding, was becoming lighter and lighter. She looked into my eyes and a tear rolled down her cheek. I was perplexed. She gradually disappeared from my arms. She slowly faded away and the last thing I could see was a hint of a smile.

My legs went weak. I stumbled and held myself up by leaning my back against the wall. The anguish and shortness of breath that I had felt when entering the house were present at that moment and it was overwhelming. My brain couldn't understand what my eyes were seeing.

Her glasses were on the nightstand and her body was lying on a small bed to the right of the room. Motionless. Half covered with the sheets and a blanket. Her hands were still holding the embroidery of the sheet.

I stumbled out of the house as best I could.

The police and ambulance arrived almost at the same time. I didn't want to go back in. I was stunned. How could I explain what had happened?

"Due to the condition of the body, she has been dead for three to four days," they informed me. "She had this in her hands."

Trembling, I grabbed the piece of paper and saw my phone number written with those crooked numbers that I remembered since I was a child.

Mariela Ivón Armando © 2024

SAMANTHA'S SWANSONG

Leaning against the alley wall Sam had one foot at knee height and was busy rolling a fatty. Just enough to take the edge off she promised herself. Her agent, or that 'lazy scumbag piece of crap that never finds me good jobs', as she liked to call him had told her to look fresh when she auditioned for the tampon ad. Fresh! Someone on her period had to look fresh because she'd just stuffed some new brand of tampon up her fanny. "Unlikely," she muttered and licked the paper to close the roll.

She lit the end and drew in a big breath of smoke, held until she couldn't any longer, then let the breath out. "I'll show them fresh alright," she murmured as she looked at the fatty with both love and disgust. Sam had tried to clean up her act many times, and she always saw this is a gateway drug, but as a gateway leading out, away from the crack and the H.

It never worked though. She had moved to London to become an actress and a model. She had done precisely two soft core porn video shoots, actually one was not so soft core, and one dodgy job for the government pretending to be a reporter interviewing some scientist, who was beyond weird, in fact he was freaky weird.

The job hadn't quite worked out how they had wanted it to, but she kept the money anyway and scored some good coke to celebrate. "Oh, I'll show them fresh," she said out loud.

She drew two more long hits off the fatty and pinched the end to save some for later. She brushed down her clothes, a smart summer dress that she had just stolen from H&M paired with a light cardigan courtesy of Zara. She had some nice, low heel, multipurpose black shoes that she had tried on about an hour ago. The salesman had run his hand way too far up her leg when he was fitting them on her foot, causing her to shudder at his nerve. When she had both shoes on, she had said she wanted to walk around the shop to feel how they fit, and 'Kevin, creepy freaking Kevin' had said OKAY. She stood and walked. She walked straight out the door and kept going to the nearest alley, when she cut through and carried on walking to Soho Square, leaving her old beaten-up trainers at the shop.

"You can keep those Kevin, maybe you can sniff them while you diddle yourself, thinking about my leg."

There was an hour to go until the audition for the kind of tampon that made you feel fresh, so she had taken the opportunity to get a minor buzz going. She had ducked into an alley, rolled one up and here she was, ready and waiting and feeling so desperate she wished she had stayed at home, with Mum and Dad and got a job at a local office. "But no, you had to be a damned actress, didn't you?" she said to herself.

She was staring blankly at the wall opposite, just lost in a feeling of melancholy when a man walked out of the wall. Not out of a doorway, or even through a window, he walked through and out of the wall.

Instantly Sam knew who it was, it was the creepy bastard she had interviewed and kinda betrayed and she had a feeling she was in for an ass kicking.

He had told Sam that he was ex-military, ex-counter terrorism and she thought that he could probably handle himself. Besides she had watched him put his hand through a table and just seen him walk out of a wall. Presumably he could reach into her chest and pull her heart out if he wanted to. Suddenly the monkey that she had earned for the job didn't seem enough.

"Damn it," she said very quietly.

"Hi Samantha," Trevor said, and he crossed the alley and stood next to her. Sam visibly shrank, shoulders hunched forward her spine compressed, and her head hung down.

"If you're going to give me a hiding can you spare the face, I've got a damn tampon audition in 40 minutes."

"A hiding? Why would I do that? You were just trying to earn a little money, and there was no harm and no foul really. In fact, it was quite good fun."

Sam let out a long slow breath and stood more upright, "If you say so Mr. Blackman."

"Oh, come on, Trevor please."

"Okay Trevor. If you say so. Trevor."

Trevor looked at the girl, feeling both sorry for her but also remembering his own tough times when he had left the Air Force. He had done his share of sleeping rough and scoring drugs too and really felt sympathy for her plight.

"Wait a minute," he said and instantly vanished then reappeared less than a second later. "Sorry to be the bearer of bad news, you don't get the tampon job, sorry Sam."

"So, it's not even worth my time going to the audition?"

"Oh, you should definitely go, you never know who you might meet there, well, I know who you'll meet there, but you don't. Yet."

Sam looked at him with a blank expression then said, "You are really, really annoying, do you know that?"

"I've been told," Trevor shrugged.

"Well, whoever told you wasn't telling you porkies, that's for sure. So, what do you want? Money? A blow job? You know us junkies, we'll do anything in the right circumstances."

"I'm going to show you something else," and he held his hand out, "Watch closely." As Sam watched his hand it was suddenly full of money, at least another few hundred, and she hadn't seen him flinch or move.

"That's some freaky David Copperfield shit right there, so I guess you don't need money, just as well really 'cause I popped the money from our interview on coke."

"Sam, I don't need, or want, anything from you, I just want to tell you something."

Sam sighed, thinking a motivational speech of some kind was about to come. Trevor relaxed against the wall a little and offered Sam the money, which she snatched out of his hand like Kung Fu Caine snatching the grasshopper from Master Kan's hand.

"Thanks."

"When we 'interviewed' I took a little look at what you would consider your future Sam, there's an infinite number of potential outcomes, some better than others, depending on choices you make in the next few hours. I already told you that you're not getting the tampon job, but I am telling you that you should go to the audition, you should try to be fresh and above all be open to new conversations. I can't say much more because of something called the Significance Algorithm, we kinda touched on that during the interview, remember?"

"Oh bless, you thought I was listening, didn't you?"

"I know some of it got through or you really are a better actress than your agent thinks you are, but that's the reason I'm here. Just a reminder, go to the audition, be fresh be open and talk to people."

"Whatever. You finished?"

"Yep." He disappeared.

"That's always going to be freaky," she said aloud to nobody.

Surprisingly Trevor reappeared about 2 seconds later and gave her a paper bag, it was full of toiletries and a whole bunch of cash.

Looking inside the bag Sam's eyes started to well with tears, "What's this for?" she asked.

"Let's just say it's some fresh start money from a fan of 'Alice's Office Adventure' a great work of art."

Sam blushed, "You saw that?"

Trevor winked and disappeared again.

Sam walked through Soho Square, she felt her shoulders pull back and for some reason she was smiling. Finding the address of the audition she buzzed through, and a receptionist ushered her through to a small studio, without even making eye contact. Sam stood still at the desk and then said, "Excuse me."

The girl looked up, "What?"

"Thank you," Sam said, smiled and walked through to the studio. A director and an assistant were sitting at a table and Sam waited until she was called to the front.

"Name?"

"Samantha Glass."

"Nice to see you Samantha, twirl for me, then say 'Ah. Fresh... please."

Sam twirled and said, "Ah. Fresh."

"Thanks, we'll let you know."

Disappointed, Sam forced a smile then started to walk out of the room. As she went through the doorway a tall woman, wearing cargo khakis and a white tee-shirt stopped her and said, "Hey, you Sam?"

"Umm, yeah?"

"Great, my name is Anita, you can call me Nits. Do you want a job?"

"What will I have to do?"

"Front for me and my colleague Simon. Too many people are looking for us, we need an agent, a fixer, a Jill of all sorts really. You come recommended."

"By Trevor?" She asked.

"How do you feel about travel Sam?"

"Well, I haven't done a whole lot err... Nits was it?"

"Yeah, Nits is fine, look put this belt on and hold my arm tight."

"Really?"

They were gone.

Peter Draper   ©   2024

FRIDAY PICK ME UP

Today is Friday, so you can absolutely say yay,

With the weekend to come, a lot of relaxation and fun to come,

With the weekend drawing near, you got nothing to fear,

It will be a long day, but after you can say yay,

It is what it is, it is what it will be,

Just know you got good friends and good karma to come,

Just chill and relax as the weekend will fly,

Because come Monday, the week has been redone,

With Saturday around the corner, there is a time to adorn her.

Time to pamper, time to chill, time to enjoy the time stand still.

Curtis L. L. Herbold © 2024

SWARMS AND PINK BUBBLES

4th January 2011.

Dear Journal.

It has been a most unsettling Christmas and start to the New Year. You know my Christmases are unsettling at the best of times but 2010 was particularly trying. I blame it all on Bella. You know all about my cousin Bella, the one who went to Florence as Isobel, Issy that is, and came back blonder, slimmer with sashaying hips and lower necklines. She tells me she has discovered style. She tells me the Italian men insisted on calling her Bella because that means beautiful in Italian and that the Italian men told her she had radiant magnetism. I know my lips are tightening and disappearing. How wonderful, I say, but are you sure that's what they were saying. After all, you don't speak the language. Perhaps they were saying something quite different, like pass the butter or we'll go halves over the dinner bill.

Bella knows this is a deliberate shot. Every year the family contributes to the cost of the Christmas lunch and in return I cook for vegans, vegetarians, and carnivores. Everybody paid up ages ago.

Not Bella.

In 2008, which became the Year of Truthfulness - you know that I had told Bella that she never repaid debts, that she couldn't be depended upon and other things as well. You are also aware that I told a lot of other people a lot of other things as well and that this led directly to 2009 being the Year of Repentance. I suppose you could summarise 2010 as the Year of Bella and Thin Lips Disappearing. Anyway, right now Bella declines my request to cut up the onions for the turkey stuffing, gets up, saunters to the door, and says, in what she probably thinks is a languid manner,

"It's sweet the way your hair frizzes in this humidity. By the way, I'm bringing Edwardo to Christmas lunch."

"Italian men don't like red hair." She flicks this at me as she goes through the door. Looking back on it, it must have been the fish and the prawns that were off. At least the vegans didn't get sick or the ones that stuck with turkey. It was a combination of two things. Bella had taken the seafood dishes out of the fridge in order to chill glasses for drinks – couldn't be bothered to use the fridge in the garage. The second thing, Cousin Jane had turned off the air conditioning – so she could save the planet. As you know, I do the cooking and Cousin Jane contributes the big house. On the plus side, Bella, who gorged on the fish and prawns she hadn't contributed to, was most definitely not radiating magnetism over the next few days. The problem was I had a bit of everything and so ended up feeling queasy as well. Still better than Bella though.

On Boxing Day, I opened her Christmas present to me. On the card she had written, Merry Christmas Poppy – Hope you enjoy the book (dear Journal, it still had the $5.00 Manager's Markdown sticker on it) and I so much hope the Creative Visualization Meditations CD will inspire you in" the field of personal growth and consciousness." The quote was directly from the CD cover.

A cup of tea, a book and then a snooze to soothing sounds and I won't be unwell anymore. The five-dollar book and I bet the marked down CD turned out to be revelations. The book is called Prey by Michael Crichton, the fellow who wrote Jurassic Park. Amongst other titles is a book called Eaters of the Dead – yuk.

Prey basically deals with the consequences of an experiment gone horribly wrong. A company under pressure to fulfil a defence contract combines the fields of nanotechnology, biotechnology and computer technology to recklessly release self-replicating entities into the environment. The self-replicating entities present as swarms. They do not stay within the strictures of self-replication but evolve beyond their original programming, which is based on the swarm intelligence of predatory animals. In short, humans become the prey, the swarms are the predators. In order to survive, the swarms eat us and in the process can replicate our shape. I become unstuck on page 260 where Michael Crichton informs me I am in fact a giant swarm.

A swarm of swarms in fact. My blood, liver and kidneys are separate body swarms. I am not solid – I am a swirling mass of cells and atoms, which are clustered together in smaller swirls of cells and atoms. All that swarming and swirling is bringing back the queasy feeling. I slide my not solid self along the bed and put my not solid head on the firm, unmoving pillow. Will self-tranquillise with comforting visualisations. I turn on the CD player.

Shakti Gawain, the visualisation guide, has a light voice and a soft American accent. She wants me to imagine there is a cord attached to my back which is making its way deep into the earth and the earth's energy will then pass through this cord and into my spine and then throughout my body. This is the grounding exercise which will keep me firmly but lovingly tethered to the earth. Trouble is I start to feel myself being dragged under the ground while a river of sludge snakes its way through and into and over my swarms within swarms, into my mouth, my nose. Am fighting for breath. Shakti tells me to envision the energies of the universe are now entering through my head and creating another energy flow. I should now be pulsating deeply with energies from below and above. All this pulsation is causing my stomach to churn.

I fast forward to track two. Shakti tells me the universe is waiting to fulfil all my desires. What I do is envision what I want; put that in a pink bubble and then let it gently waft away. The universe will then see to it that my wish will come true. This is called manifesting. I concentrate on making a pink bubble and doze off. And dream. My swarms turn into demented antlike figures bent on manifesting revenge for bad fish and prawns. They blow thousands and thousands of pink bubbles which they burst with sharp little pincers. My stomach overfills with sticky sloshing liquid, and I feel the hot, sour sting of bile at the back of my throat. I wake up just as my stomach heaves and lurch to the bathroom with murderous thoughts toward Bella and Cousin Jane.

6th January

Bella's birthday. I send her two books by Michael Crichton, Eaters of the Dead (hard to find) and Next which deals with the following questions – is a loved one missing body parts, are blondes becoming extinct and has a human already cross-bred with a monkey? I write on the card. Dear Bella, Happy Birthday. Don't worry about the blondes becoming extinct – I'm sure he meant only the natural ones. (Just joking) Love Poppy

8th January

Edwardo rings. How am I? Wanted to ring before but heard I was ill. What have I been doing? I tell him about Prey. He's fascinated. I tell him about trying meditation. He's charmed. I am radiating magnetism without trying. Would I like to go to Florence and cook in his restaurant? I would be the Elizabeth Rossetti of his kitchen and his heart.

I know three things about Elizabeth Rossetti. She was a talented artist. She had fabulous red hair. And when she died, her broken-hearted husband secretly placed in her casket, the collection of poems he had prepared for publication. Six years later he had the coffin hauled up; the rotting notebook of poems was removed and down went Elizabeth again. So, I'm onto Edwardo, but. After all, Florence is Florence. I ring Cousin Jane and have a long chat. Slip in that Edwardo is mad about my red hair. He is bowled over by my blend of scientific knowledge and spirituality. He has invited me to Florence.

I smirk when I put the phone down.

Everyone knows Cousin Jane always tells Bella everything.

Susannah Thompson © 2024

LITTLE TRUDY'S SECRETS

Trudy was sharing her peanut butter sandwich with her fat black cat Midnight, who was crouched at her feet. She had to be careful that mommy didn't catch them. Mommy said Midnight was too fat and shouldn't eat all the fun food that Trudy fed her.

Working on getting the peanut butter off the top of her mouth and on the outside of her lips, Trudy let the cat work to get the soft goodie off her finger that she was holding down below the table. Trudy used only her right-hand finger, as mommy had warned her about her left hand.

Mommy said when she was older, they would take the time to show her how to use both her hands, especially her left hand properly. Right now, everyone was too busy for special lessons and secrets.

She felt a tiny bit guilty, not minding mommy, but Midnight was the only other person who knew her special secret, and the big fat black cat kept her secrets. Midnight never told anyone when Trudy went out into the woods and took her shirt off and let her wings out to fly. She hid her wings from everyone, even mommy because no one else had wings.

Trudy had to be more careful now, even though she loved the feeling of the freedom she got from the wings. She wasn't sure where they went when her wings disappeared. She knew that when mommy helped her bathe, there were no marks in her back. She was glad that her wings were hidden because she wanted something unique that was all her own.

She now had a baby brother, so she no longer got all the attention from her parents. They were busy, and this meant it might take them longer to teach her all the things she needed to know, as she was growing up. After all, she was four years old now. She needed to act like a big girl.

She was going to have to learn how to take care of her little brother and protect him. After all, they were entirely different, and it was necessary to keep away from the outsiders.

She slipped out the back door, letting Midnight lead the way into the woods on their usual path. When they got deep into the forest, she was free.

She smiled as she brushed against the pine needles with her wings out, taking her higher than her small legs would let her climb.

Up in the sweet-smelling air, she heard Midnight hiss a warning and looked down to see her black friend hunched down, all hairs standing upright.

Trudy slowly used her wings to come down to see a boy sitting in the leaves and dead pine needles, next to a small spotted dog. He was holding a leash on the puppy who seemed happy to see her. The little dog looked so friendly and panted, as it looked over at Midnight. The dog looked like it wanted to play with the fat black cat, but Midnight was not sure what to make about the little dog on the leash.

She had no choice, but to come down, as the boy was looking at her. She tucked her wings before she dropped, hoping he thought she had scrambled up a tree. She grabbed her shirt and put it on, turning her bare back to let him see it without wings.

Perhaps she had fooled him, and he just thought she had climbed a tree. She had her fingers crossed as she turned and knelt down next to Midnight to calm her friend. It now looked like Midnight might want to be a companion with the little dog, if he would understand that the cat was boss.

"I'm Ben. I live down the road. I play in these woods to hide from the big boys who are bullies. I bet you do the same thing."

Trudy looked around.

"No, you're the first kid I've seen. My mommy doesn't let me play beyond our property, so I haven't met anyone else. No one is supposed to come back here to my daddy's property."

Trudy sat down on the damp ground, and Midnight was settling down in her lap. Mommy always said she needed to be polite. "My name is Trudy. You have a nice doggy. Will his hurt my cat?"

Actually, the whole time she had watched the boy with the dog on the leash, the dog had sat with its tail wagging in the needles on the ground. The dog didn't look very dangerous. In fact, it looked cute, almost like one of her stuffed toys.

The boy glanced around. "We could be friends."

Mommy had said to be polite, but she didn't say anything about friends. "I don't think my mommy will let me have friends. We never have anyone over at our house."

The boy looked over his shoulder. "No one in our little area has friends over. That is why the bullies like to pick on all of us. We are all different on this edge of town."

Trudy shrugged. "I'm not different. I'm four years old. Next year I can go to school for half a day."

The little boy smiled. "You think they will let you go to school with those wings?"

Trudy didn't want to cry, but why was the boy being so mean? She pulled Midnight close to hug the cat. Midnight pushed out two paws and curled them, loved to be cuddled by Trudy.

The boy scooted closer. "I didn't mean to hurt your feelings. I just want to be friends. I have a secret too."

The boy leaned forward until he was on his knees. The little dog backed away, as far as it could on the leash and whined. The boy was closing his eyes, and it looked like he was pushing something really hard like he had to go to the potty.

Suddenly his face changed. His nose stretched and grew, and hair began to sprout out to cover his skin. His ears stood up, above his head, covered with brown fur. His eyes glistened in a blue colour, like the wolves she saw on TV.

Midnight rose up, all protective cat, claws out, teeth showing and the hair on her back straight up.

There was a deep sigh from the wolf face, and with strange sounds, the face returned into the boy.

"See, now we both have a secret. We can share and stay friends."

His little dog had settled down and quit whining, yet it stayed away from the boy. It looked at her with sad eyes on the end of its short leash.

Trudy shook her head. "I just don't think my mommy will allow it. Sorry."

Trudy stood up and looking in the boy's eyes. She waved her left hand at him. It was the one mommy told her to be careful how she pointed with it.

She said, "Go away." With a puff, the boy disappeared. It was just like when she made the mad dog disappear. She had also made the tree knocked down from a storm disappear and some junk in the forest where she played. They all disappeared and were out of the family's way.

Walking back to the house, she could smell the cupcakes her mother had been baking. She smiled as she thought she now had two small friends to sneak treats to under the table.

The little dog trotted along at her side without the leash. He never whined after she took it off his neck and he licked her hand in what she thought was a thank you. Midnight led the way home, trying to prove that as a cat, she was the mistress of the household.

Mom greeted her at the door. "And who is this?"

"Mommy, this is Midnight's friend. She wants us to keep him."

Mother looked down at the little dog that was being ignored by the fat cat and laughed.

"Well, we can't turn down Midnight, can we? How about some milk and a cupcake?"

Trudy washed her hands and climbed up on a stool. She watched her mom settle her new baby brother in a basket, as she ate.

"So, Trudy, what did you do today in the woods. You were careful, weren't you?"

"Yes, mommy." Trudy let some crumbs fall to the floor. "I played with a friend and then imagined him away. Midnight liked the dog, and I allowed her to bring him home. He is small and won't eat much."

"Okay, we can keep the puppy. But if a real person comes into the woods, come home immediately and tell us. Remember, we are a little different from the folks out there in the world, so we can't mix with them."

"Yes, mommy." Trudy smiled down at the dog, knowing he was happier with her and Midnight than he had been with the boy who scared him when the boy changed into a wolf. The dog had told her with his eyes that he was afraid that someday the wolf would kill him. But he knew that Midnight would never hurt him and he shared the crumbs on the floor with his new fat friend.

Mommy added a larger water bowl before she turned to the baby brother. Life was good in this house of secrets.

M. Garnet © 2024

SORGHUM COUNTRY

This is my kind of truckie. He picked me up on a lonely stretch of the highway, a raised eyebrow his only enquiry about what I was doing in the middle of nowhere. Nor did he offer any comment when I neglected to inform him or even inquire into his own destination.

Truckies must be used to the loneliness of the road, but for some the arrival of a pair of ears unties their tongues, and they feel a need for conversation. This one looked like he would welcome silence as much as speech. So, he communed with the road before him while I communed with the land it passed through, and our peace seemed as much a bond of companionship as tales and laughter.

But it was a melancholy peace, at least for me. There is something about passing through such empty country that makes me feel the loneliness of its inhabitants, scattered among the vast fields of grain and cattle, little islands of people in their remote farmhouses. I know of their existence, but not of their hearts or minds. As I pass by their brief domains, I know that, as intense as our lives are to ourselves, with all the passions and fears, loves and hates, ambitions or laziness that are the common heritage of our kind, nothing of us exists in the mind of the other.

Just like the truckie and me, I reflect. Lives briefly intersecting, never knowing more than that raw fact of simultaneous breath, never to meet again, never to learn each other's fates. Perhaps never to think of each other again.

In the distance I see a derelict farmhouse, set a little back from the highway among some trees. Its beams show stark against the sky: a skeleton still half-dressed by walls that once protected the warm lives inside, but now are nothing but their slumped shrouds and silent memorial. Yet it must have been the heat haze, or maybe just a projection of my own mood, for as we come closer, I realise it is not derelict at all. The white walls look well maintained, its garden has flowers somehow defying the harsh sun, and a metal sign hangs by the roadside, tersely declaring: 'Rooms'.

I had no plans other than a vague goal of reaching some town or other, but something about this place calls to me, as it shimmers ahead like some vision of the past. I ask the driver to let me off here. He offers me a sidewise glance. "Are you sure, mate? There's nothing much around here. Happy to drop you off at the next town or so instead."

I shake my head, and he shrugs, as if leaving me to my fate. He drops me off at the roadside some distance past the homestead, then his rig rumbles off into the heat haze, until nothing is left to mark its existence but a haze of gritty red dust and a faint whiff of diesel.

I walk back toward the house, which continues to play with my eyes as the sun beats down on my head. It had looked derelict, then white and elegant, timeless; but now as I stand in the heat gazing at it from the roadside, it shows as faded and worn, the metal sign now tarnished, squeaking gently as it rocks in the soft breeze. Once the house must have been grand, a place full of wealth and the laughter of children, but the past glory which sang to me is long departed. I put my duffel down and stand there for a while looking at it, contemplating my prospects.

I gaze both ways down the empty highway. I shrug, running my finger through the sweaty dust under my collar, then pick up my duffel and stroll up the driveway to the house. I climb the stairs to the front door and, taking the mat's proclaimed 'Welcome' at its word, let myself into an interior as cool as it is gloomy.

I expected to find its owner some matching relic, perhaps an old lady possessed of the same faded elegance as her hotel. So, I am surprised to encounter a young woman, slender and attractive, dressed in a simple white gown, glossy chestnut hair framing a face with grey eyes, startling in their intensity.

I ask her whether I can rent a room and she nods once. I ask her name but she only smiles, pointing to her lips and throat and shaking her head, as if indicating she cannot speak. She points to the register, pens and a folder of information.

I look around the hall, wondering what I am doing here. There are no brochures touting the local tourist attractions, but I guess that if this place is here, there must be something nearby. Maybe horses for riding, though I had seen none. Perhaps a river or a lake where a man can fish or swim. I glance at my hostess, and it is if she can feel my reluctance to stay, for her eyes contain a strange pleading, though she makes no effort to plead more directly. I smile at her and fill out the register, and she smiles back.

She leads me up the wooden staircase to the first storey, explaining with gestures which room is mine and where the amenities are. I ask about dinner, and she holds up six fingers. Then she lets me into my room and leaves me to my privacy.

My room has a high ceiling and a slowly moving fan dancing with even slower moving flies. There is no air conditioning, but I have the fan and the large window. I do not mind the heat.

Curious, I look through my lodgings. Some old clothes still hang in the cupboard, mouldering in the dark as they have done for years, perhaps more years than I have been alive. Among some ancient papers in a drawer, I find an envelope loosely tied with a black ribbon. Perhaps it is rude to open it, but if it was meant to be private, why would it be left here for any stranger to find? In any case, like the house itself it calls to me. Inside is nothing but a photograph. It is old, black and white faded to yellow, and shows a young woman. She is simply but well dressed and looks directly at the camera with a faint smile. Around her neck hangs a pendant with a stone, from its shade

I guess a sapphire. The woman looks remarkably like my hostess, so I guess she is some ancestor, long dead now.

There is a knock at my door. When I open it, outside is a tray of hot food and a bottle of cold beer beaded with moisture, but my hostess did not stay to greet or join me.

I eat alone in my room. The food is simple, but tasty enough and filling. When I am finished, I place the tray outside and close my door. I gaze again at the old photo, and, looking into the girl's face, I wonder what happened to her, whether she had a happy life; whether she married, had children, and perhaps my strange hostess yet carries part of her life within her. Though the black ribbon gives me unease, and I suspect a more tragic end greeted that wistful smile, so alive with uncertain hope. But whether she lived a long life or a short one, I know that, like her once home, only echoes now remain of her life and joys and sorrows. I feel a strange affinity with her, and sit at my window, contemplating her. She is like the people I passed in the distance, only more so: separated by not only miles but years.

I sit there a long time, absorbed in her face and the rhythm of the land. This is sorghum country, and the grain slowly ripples in the haze as the lowering sun beats down uncaring. An eagle circles lazily far above, perhaps hoping for an incautious rabbit. A police car hares along the road without stopping, as indifferent to my presence as the sky.

I close my eyes, and a young woman haunts dreams of long ago.

Then something awakens me from the dream, and I am startled to see my hostess in my room, looking so much like my dream that for a moment I do not know whether I am indeed awake or still sleeping. She gazes at me with an odd hunger in her eyes then smiles gently. I smile back, uncertain what else to do. Then she steps forward, shrugging her gown off her shoulders, watching me nervously. Whatever she sees in my face emboldens her, for she leans over and kisses me long and gently on the lips. When she lifts her head I look into her eyes, which show fear, excitement and a driving passion that will not be denied. My own desire awakes, unable to refuse her even if I wished, and I reach for her, pulling her down to me. She is soft in my arms, almost insubstantial, and I can tell that this is something she has never done. Then when we are finished, for the first time a sound escapes from her lips, a sigh speaking of a need long desired, long absent, now finally reached; but a breath so soft I cannot be sure it is her and not merely the rustling of the sorghum in the breeze.

When I look at her, she is already asleep, a soft smile on her lips, a smile of release, contentment and fulfilment. I feel an unaccounted tenderness for this girl, and I hold her in my arms as I too fall asleep.

I wake to the mournful sound of crows in the rafters. The rising sun casts shadows of the naked beams above my head across my naked body and the decaying mattress upon which I lie. I dress, looking around at the ruins of the house, then carefully descend the rotting staircase until I reach the outside. I look at the collapsing building, the dry sticks where flowers once bloomed, and down the driveway the remains of a rusty sign lying in the dust.

I lift my hand in farewell, though to whom, I do not know. Then I turn and walk away.

I wonder when the next truck will be along.

Robin Craig © 2024

SIMPLY TO FLY

The beach glimmered in the sun as the boy slowly crept through the coarse sea grass growing tall among the dunes. He carried a large net like those used by fishermen to land salmon as they trolled the Pacific Northwest coastline. When he reached the beach, the boy saw a seagull pecking a sand dollar. Cat-like he crept…moving closer; he leaped, capturing the gull in the tangled web. Holding the squawking young gull tightly between his legs, he untangled the thrashing wings and feet, dug in his pocket, and removed a ball of string. After he tied the string haphazardly to a webbed foot, the frantic bird was released. The gull, believing itself free from the trap, soared into the sky. The freedom was short-lived. The boy roughly yanked on the string and started to run. The gull fell hard and was dragged along the sand through clumps of grass. Quickly taking flight the confused gull was again pulled back; slammed against the sand; again trying to fly—again and again. The brutal game continued until, at last, the string gave way from the bleeding leg and the frantic gull, feeling the constraint gone, ran into the ocean and quickly swam to deep water.

*　*　*

As the sleeping seagull bobbed over the ground swells in the surf, an errant breaker splashed over his body waking him from his nap. He opened his eyes and ruffled his feathers. Looking ashore, he saw a fledging gull standing alone. She was lovely and delicate, silvery wing tips against her white body. In his rush to swim to shore, he splashed water on his back. The sun shining on his feathers made him appear like a white knight coming to her rescue.

"Scree," he squawked wading through the surf.

"Chee," she cooed as she pranced before him. His strong white back was sleek and shiny and the feathers at the top of his head had a bit of a curl.

"I'm Gull." He puffed out his chest.

"Chee." She chirped. "My mama flew away. Help me find her."

"Scree! Fly?"

Chee bobbed her head.

Gull quickly pulled his scarred leg up under his feathered belly. "Stay here. You don't need to fly."

"Don't fly. Why?"

"Flying gulls are a low-life species. They eat garbage thrown from boats and get in big squawks, fighting over it." Gull swaggered before her, kicking up mounds of sand. "I'm clever. I hunt for food."

"Mussels?" She cawed excitedly.

"Yes, and fish that swim far out to sea."

"It's scary to swim too far."

"That's because you're only a she-gull." He gazed down on her shining head. "I'll bring you fish."

A small flock of gulls flew over them and Gull put his curved bill far into the air. He squawked out a raucous commentary on the way of life of other seagulls. "Squawk, screech, squawk." Gazing at Chee from the corner of his eye, his beak curved into a smug grin.

For the next several days, Gull stayed close to Chee chasing away other gulls that came their way. Having established his territory, he approached Chee standing in the bubbling surf watching the gentle waves washing against the sand. Cautiously, he moved closer and gave her a soft peck on her head. She placed her beak into his downy neck.

The sun had turned into a fiery orange ball as it seemed to vanish into the watery depths of the gray ocean. Their tail feathers could be seen bobbing up and down as four webbed feet piled up little mounds of sand as they scurried toward an abandoned pier located in the distance.

For several days, Chee and Gull enjoyed discovering each other as they frolicked on the beach, scuffling in the sand and splashing in the water, experiencing the mating ritual of seagulls.

One evening, as they stood at the end of the pier looking out over the formidable ocean, Chee said: "Let's fly fast and capture the sun. I don't want the day to end."

"Don't be stupid. Scree. You can't stop the sun from setting."

"I want to fly. We have wings." Standing tall with her back arched and her wings spread wide, she demonstrated how. "Let's go!"

"Squawk! Forget it. We are safe on the ground." He limped toward their nest.

After that incident, Chee didn't seem to want to leave her nest. Gull thought she was sad because he wouldn't let her fly. He brought many purple mussels for her to nibble on, but she ignored him. One day, he heard Chee cawing and thought she was in danger. He ran to the nest but discovered she was just excited …and proud. She had laid three eggs.

She patiently sat on her expectant offspring, until one day, boredom took over. She stood up and looked down at the three warm eggs. "Gull, sit for a while."

"No. Hatching eggs is she-gull work." He squawked as he strutted away. A little while later, he brought back a juicy morsel of food and dropped it in the nest.

Chee's diligence was finally rewarded when one afternoon, she felt a stirring under her bottom. She jumped up.

Gull heard her excited screech and came running to the nest. They watched as their chicks pecked through the shells and came tumbling out as wet little balls of gray fuzz, their bills opened wide, peeping for their first meal. Gull nuzzled Chee as they beheld their chicks.

Chee cooed to her chicks and rubbed her bill along their soft fuzzy backs. They looked at her with half opened eyes and snuggled deep in the warm nest. Their bellies were full with the food she had thrust deep in their throats. Having responsibility for her chicks, keeping them warm, fed and hidden from predatory animals, Chee was exhausted, but she knew she didn't dare ask Gull for help, convinced he'd again tell her it was she-gull's work. She wiggled and settled herself over the chicks.

A few weeks later, Gull became impatient with Chee's devotion to the chicks and her avoidance of him. "Chicks need to leave the nest," he squawked one morning, waking her up.

Chee moved her head from under her wing and yawned. She was surprised to see him standing over her. "No. They're mine."

"They have to leave the nest and learn how to take care of themselves."

One of the chicks had moved out into the nest. She pulled him back under her wing. "They are too little to..."

"Too little, that's all I ever hear," he squawked. "You're hopeless." He thrust his webbed foot out, kicking some of the twigs loose from the nest.

Chee's feathers drooped. She snuggled against the chicks and watched Gull swim out to sea. In her heart, she knew Gull was right; the time had come.

The sun had risen over the dunes when she encouraged the chicks to wake up and follow her to the beach. First, she showed them how to find food and they learned how to grab quickly to keep the other birds from snatching their prize. Next, she knew she had to teach them to fly. She obeyed Gull by not flying herself (except when she was sure he couldn't see her), but her chicks were a different matter.

"Watch mama-gull. You must learn to fly." The chick's eyes were wide as they watched Chee run down the beach and with her wings out she took off from the sand and flew a few feet, circled above and landed near the chicks.

"You try, just like mamma did."

Without hesitation, the chicks followed her lead and before long, each one was able to fly. For the rest of the day, they all practiced flying, having a wonderful time.

A few days later, Chee stood with her fledgling chicks at the end of the pier. Gull watched them from the surf below.

She put her wings around each of her chicks for the last time. She and Gull watched as the three young gulls flew over the beach to vanish behind the high dunes in the distance.

The shoreline was littered with smooth pebbles, broken seashells and kelp incrusted with sand and fleas. An unrelenting drizzle surrounded Chee's mature body. She knew she would miss the chicks, but that could be bearable if only she and Gull could be content with each other. Chee finally admitted that she could not truly be happy unless she could experience all life had to offer. Her love of Gull was true but she didn't know if she could continue to make a sacrifice and not fly, except by deception.

Her thoughts became more tormented. He needs me. All he has is his pride. What will happen to me if I leave? I am safe here. What is it like out there? If only we could explore together.

Chee had been unable to understand why Gull did not want to fly. Every gull she had ever seen had been able to fly. Did his mother never teach him? Maybe he would let her teach him how, like she taught the chicks. The solution for Chee's problem now seemed so simple. She would teach Gull to fly, to swoop and ride the air currents, just as she had taught her chicks. She was excited as she planned her strategy.

Chee snuggled against Gull's chest feathers and gave him little pecks under his curved bill. They walked along quietly for a few minutes. Chee danced in front of him, causing him to stop in mid-stride. "Are you angry because I taught our chicks how to fly?"

"No. They had to leave home. There is only enough food for you and me."

"I want to fly too."

"NEVER! I won't allow it!" He batted at her with his wing.

"But we are meant to fly…" Chee danced away from him.

"No!" He squawked loudly. "I know what is best." In his agitation, he frantically ruffled his feathers.

"I'll show you how," she screed as she started to run from him. Chee's webbed feet were throwing up puffs of sand as she took off in the air. She climbed higher and higher, circling above him.

He looked up. The sun shining on her silver-white wings reminded him of the stars in the midnight sky. Her eyes sparkled and the smile on her beak was beautiful. He stood quietly and watched her soar through the air. She gracefully glided over the sea coming to rest upon the water, sending ripples in her wake as she swam toward him. Gull was standing on one foot at the edge of the surf watching foam sink into the sand.

"Will Gull try?" She nudged against him.

He shoved his chest out. "You're not better than me! I can fly. I'll show you!"

He strutted from her, and then began to run along the beach, spreading his wings wide. The air quickly lifted him several feet off the ground. He flapped his powerful wings, flying higher and higher. He looked down, closed his eyes and remembered being pulled to earth. He was falling, down… down, his wings floating uselessly above him. He landed hard, his bill sticking into the sand. Stunned for a few seconds, he jumped up and frantically shook the sand from his feathers. He quietly walked away, his head held low.

Chee was sad for causing Gull this humiliation. Deciding she would never again suggest flying, she resigned herself to her fate. She followed him to their nest. As a concession to herself, she decided to fly no matter how Gull felt about it. Surprisingly, he no longer objected.

During Chee's first flying adventure, she couldn't stop looking at the sights of the landscape below, the tall fir trees and narrow roads winding through the mountains. The sun shining on the water looked like a million diamonds dazzling her vision. The warm air currents allowed her to relax and glide as she continued to gaze at this new world below. As the day progressed, she became lonely, thinking how wonderful it would be to have Gull fly by her side. Reluctantly, she turned south and headed back toward her home.

She flew everyday now, thoroughly enjoying her newfound independence, but it was impossible for her to totally disregard her old habits. No matter how far she ventured during the day, she would always return to Gull so they could hunt for food together in the evening.

One day she saw four other gulls flying above. She flew close to them and screed loudly, "Chee."

"Where's your mate?" One of the gulls screeched.

"Below." The small flocked could see the lone Gull sitting on the dock with his head held high.

"Is he crippled?" Cawed one of the female gulls.

"No. He is very strong."

As the day progressed, she observed something curious. There were no cross squawks, and she watched in wonder at the affection the gulls showed toward their mates. A plan was beginning to develop in her mind. She would invite her new friends to meet Gull. Surely, he would like them as much as she. Perhaps they all could persuade Gull to join their flock.

Her desire was not to be realized as Gull's behavior toward the flying gulls was rude and objectionable. He lost no time criticizing Chee as a mate.

The next day was difficult for Chee as she flew near her new friends; however, their sympathy for her was real. "Chee, don't put up with Gull when he squawks at you," one of the female gulls told Chee.

"Yes, Chee, squawk back at him." One of the male birds cawed. "Let him know you don't like it."

Chee was afraid to squawk at Gull anymore, remembering last night when he pecked at her back so hard it brought blood to her white feathers.

Several days later, Chee's friends introduced her to other seagulls and she was accepted as a part of the larger flock located near a bustling marina. While Chee basked in positive attention, gaining much needed self-assurance, her relationship with Gull deteriorated at an alarming rate.

One day the flock flew over Gull's deserted pier on their way to meet a passing fishing trawler. Chee's silver wing tips were easily picked out among the flock. The sight of her with the high-flying gulls was more than Gull could tolerate. With his beak high in the air, he screeched in his loudest, most domineering squawk, "Chee! Come down!"

She saw her mate standing on the dock with his head held high. The other gulls continued with their flight. She descended slowly, landing gracefully to stand in front of Gull.

"Chee is a bad mate. Selfish gull! SQUAWK. I hate high-flying gulls. Stay home where you belong! SQUAWK, SCREECH." His caw became louder and louder as he continued to rant at her in his most contemptible manner.

Quietly she stared at him as if seeing him for the first time. She looked down at her feet, letting his anger roll off her feathers. She had always felt guilty he wasn't happy. She now understood his unhappiness was his problem, and not hers.

When he finally simmered down, she cooed a mournful sigh. "I don't know how to make you happy." She spread her wings in a questioning manner. Her head was bowed. He looked at her, confused by her calm, non-defensive manner.

"I have to fly," she squawked, pulling her head back up. "I can't live unless I fly. I don't know what else I can do." She reached out her wings.

Gull was breathing heavily as he stared at her. They remained silent as they continued to look at each other.

He started to walk toward her. "Don't go. I will change. Scree..." Chee backed away from him.

"It doesn't matter. Too late." She backed further away. Sadly, she looked into his eyes one last time and turning quickly, she ran to the edge of the pier and took flight, her wings gracefully taking her high into the air.

He watched as the sun glittered off her feathers, a single silhouette flying high and alone. He walked to the end of the pier, still watching the speck in the distance. Suddenly, he was furious. He began to flap his wings.

"She can't do this to me!" He flapped his powerful wings faster and took flight. He climbed higher in the air keeping his eyes on the dot in the distance. Looking down, he stared at the world below but continued to flap his wings.

"Chee! I'm flying! I'm free! Scree, Scree," he cried excitedly. Discovering how simple the task, he continued to pump his wings, shortening the distant between him and his mate. Then it dawned on him what he was doing. The bitter bile of pride came into his throat. Banking one wing, making a wide arc, he changed his course and slowly flew in another direction.

Deena Lindstedt © 2002

REMNANT

The Oldie Curiosity Shop differed from the other antique, bric-a-brac and charity stores that lined the seafront in the rapidly fading village of Underconstumple in the designated tourist zone known as the Fossil Coast, in that it rented out, by the hour, old people with stories to tell, or as they liked to call it, remnants from remnants.

For a modest sum, you could rent a desiccated, but nonetheless living and mostly coherent, octogenarian who in a previous time had held an important role in the community and, as they talked, customers would wonder at how such people ever existed, let alone earned a living.

Shirlene Hardcastle (Shirlene Farquhar as was) would have people gape mouthed as she related how she gave birth to five children, never had a paid job, made all the family's clothes on a cantankerous Singer sewing machine that she'd bought second-hand, cooked meals on something she called a stove and they would guffaw in disbelief when she'd say she couldn't remember ever being unhappy.

Ernie, the last of the Youngblood clan from Tantanoola, would regale his customers with stories of repairing cars that people had to drive themselves and constantly refill with something called petrol; when he added that these cars sometimes cost more than a house and had a propensity to kill their owners with little warning, skeptical eyebrows would collide with the ceiling.

Marilyn Burnside specialised in describing how people used to be required to travel many miles to work in buildings called offices and spend their days typing on something called a keyboard and communicate with people in other offices with an instrument with a cord attached called a telephone, all for the purpose of selling things to other people who worked in offices, just like them.

But the star attraction was Bill Barnes, who would show them things called books, consisting of printed words on paper made from trees, that people would buy to keep in their homes and sometimes read more than once, a fact that stunned his customers almost as much as the fact that you couldn't talk to them and get a response (although some wondered if they were an early version of a teenager).

Doug Jacquier © 2024

LINDA IN THE VILLAGE

Linda had always been a city girl. The noise, the hustle and bustle, the towering skyscrapers, and the crowded streets were all she had ever known. But after years of working long hours in a high-stress job, she felt drained and disconnected. She longed for a change, a break from the daily grind. When her friend Sarah invited her to spend a few months in her hometown village, Linda hesitated at first. She had never been to a village before and didn't know what to expect. But the idea of a slower pace of life appealed to her, so she agreed.

Sarah's village, Mbinga, was nestled in a lush valley surrounded by rolling hills and dense forests. As Linda stepped off the bus, the fresh air hit her like a wave. It was cool, crisp, and carried the scent of wildflowers and damp earth. She took a deep breath, feeling an unfamiliar sense of peace settle over her.

"Welcome to Mbinga!" Sarah greeted her with a wide smile. "You're going to love it here. Come on, let's go to the house."

Linda followed Sarah down a narrow, winding path that led to a small cottage made of mud bricks and thatched with palm leaves. The simplicity of the home was a stark contrast to Linda's modern apartment in the city, but it had a charm that she couldn't deny.

"This is beautiful," Linda said, looking around.

"I knew you'd like it," Sarah replied, beaming with pride. "Come inside, and I'll show you around."

The interior was cozy and warm. Handmade rugs covered the floors, and the walls were adorned with colorful tapestries. A small fireplace sat in one corner, and a wooden table with mismatched chairs occupied the center of the room. The kitchen was modest, with a clay stove and shelves lined with jars of spices and dried herbs.

"This is lovely, Sarah," Linda said, feeling more at ease than she had in months.

"Thank you! Now, let me show you the garden," Sarah said, leading Linda to the back of the house.

The garden was a burst of colors—rows of vegetables, herbs, and flowers. Bees buzzed lazily from blossom to blossom, and butterflies flitted through the air.

"You grow all of this yourself?" Linda asked, amazed.

"Yes, it's therapeutic," Sarah said, kneeling to pluck a ripe tomato. "Here, try this."

Linda took the tomato, biting into its juicy flesh. The flavor was unlike anything she had ever tasted—fresh, sweet, and full of life.

"This is incredible," she said, savoring the taste.

"That's the magic of nature," Sarah replied with a smile. "Come on, let's go meet some of the villagers."

As they walked through the village, Linda noticed how different everything was from the city. People moved at a leisurely pace, stopping to chat with each other. Children played in the streets, their laughter echoing through the air. There were no blaring horns, no crowds jostling for space. Instead, there was a sense of community and harmony that Linda found refreshing.

Sarah introduced her to several villagers—Elder Musa, the wise old man who knew everything about the village's history; Mama Aisha, the baker whose bread was famous for miles; and young David, who ran the local market with his father. Each person greeted Linda with warmth and curiosity.

"Welcome to Mbinga, Linda," Elder Musa said, his eyes twinkling with kindness. "We hope you find peace and happiness here."

"Thank you," Linda replied, feeling genuinely touched. "I think I already am."

Over the next few weeks, Linda settled into village life. She helped Sarah in the garden, learned to cook traditional dishes, and even tried her hand at pottery. The villagers welcomed her with open arms, and she quickly became a part of the community. She spent her days exploring the surrounding hills, sitting by the river, and enjoying the beauty of nature. For the first time in years, Linda felt truly alive.

One morning, as Linda was walking to the market, she noticed a group of children gathered around something on the ground. Curious, she approached and saw that they were playing with a small, injured bird.

"What happened?" she asked.

"We found it like this," one of the boys said, looking up at her with wide eyes. "Can you help it?"

Linda knelt down, gently picking up the bird. Its wing was twisted, and it chirped weakly.

"Let's take it to Sarah," Linda said. "She'll know what to do."

They hurried back to Sarah's house, where Sarah examined the bird with a practiced eye.

"It's not too bad," she said. "We just need to splint its wing and let it rest."

Linda watched as Sarah skillfully bandaged the bird's wing and placed it in a small basket with some soft cloth.

"Thank you, Sarah," Linda said. "You're always so good with these things."

"It's just a matter of patience and care," Sarah replied. "You have that in you too, Linda."

Linda smiled, feeling a sense of accomplishment. As she cared for the bird over the next few days, she found herself reflecting on her life. In the city, she had always been rushing, always stressed, always trying to prove herself. But here, in the village, she had learned the value of slowing down, of taking time to appreciate the small things.

One evening, as Linda sat by the river watching the sunset, Sarah joined her.

"You seem happy," Sarah said, sitting down beside her.

"I am," Linda replied. "I didn't realize how much I needed this."

"I'm glad," Sarah said. "You've brought a lot of joy to the village. Everyone loves having you here."

"I love being here," Linda said. "It's like I've found a part of myself I didn't know was missing."

They sat in comfortable silence, watching the sky turn shades of orange and pink. The river flowed gently, and the sound of crickets filled the air.

"I don't know if I can go back to the city," Linda admitted after a while. "Life there feels so empty now."

"You don't have to," Sarah said. "You can stay here as long as you like. Mbinga is your home now, too."

Linda felt a surge of gratitude. She had found a place where she belonged, where she was accepted and loved. The village had taught her the importance of community, of living in harmony with nature, and of finding joy in the simple things.

As the days turned into weeks, Linda became more involved in village life. She helped organize festivals, taught children how to read, and even started a small pottery class. The villagers appreciated her enthusiasm and dedication, and she felt a deep sense of fulfillment.

One day, Elder Musa approached Linda with a request.

"We're planning to build a new community center," he said. "Would you be willing to help us with the planning?"

"Of course!" Linda replied, excited by the idea.

The project brought the entire village together. Everyone pitched in, offering their skills and time. Linda worked closely with the builders, designing a space that would serve as a gathering place for the community. It was hard work, but the sense of accomplishment and unity made it worthwhile.

As the new community center was completed, the village held a celebration. There was music, dancing, and food. Linda stood back, watching the villagers laugh and enjoy themselves. She felt a deep sense of pride and joy. Mbinga had become her home, and its people her family.

"Thank you for bringing me here, Sarah," Linda said, turning to her friend.

"I didn't bring you here," Sarah replied with a smile. "You found your way here. And we're all better for it."

Linda realized then that her time in the village had changed her in ways she never expected. She had discovered a new way of living, one that valued connection, compassion, and simplicity. Mbinga had given her a new purpose and a sense of belonging that she had never felt before.

As the night wore on and the stars filled the sky, Linda knew that she had found her true home. The city was no longer a place she longed for. Here, in the village, she had found happiness, peace, and herself. And she knew that this was just the beginning of a new and beautiful chapter in her life.

Damian Nakare II © 2024

THE SIBLINGS THREE: A TRAGEDY IN TWO PARTS

PART II: DARK EYES, DARK HEARTS

The siblings three,
so sad and empty.
Can't fix their own lives,
won't pull themselves free.

The elder sister:
the source of it all.
Experimentation.
So many did fall.

Behold all the carnage,
behold all the death.
You're wrong, older sister.
You're wrong.

The shy middle brother:
an artist, a brain.
No need to try harder,
no need to abstain.

Get out of your bedroom,

get out of your house.
You're wrong, middle brother.
You're wrong.

The kind younger brother:
we all let him slide.
Throughout his life
he got a free ride.

Snap out of your fancy,
snap out of your lies.
You're wrong, little brother.
You're wrong.

The siblings three,
so jaded and hazy.
Won't take that first step,
can't let go of ease.

Peter McCollum © 2024

AUTUMN RIVER

On a wide open blue beautiful lake on an early autumn afternoon the leaves had started to change colors and were just starting to blow. A man by the name of Henry Henderson was out on a kayak trip that he had been on for five days now. He decided he would stop for a rest and maybe a bite to eat, he had packed himself plenty of food and picked lots of naturals along the way through his travels. Although he had come a long way he had still anticipated on five more days as he was travelling to Big Pine Lake. He had to travel several rivers and waterways to get there, he had no urgent business to attend to it was just a great sight he had heard of but had not discovered for himself. Henry was the kind of guy who wanted to explore and discover whatever he could on his adventures.

He started traveling along the coastline, looking for a place to rest. He eventually came to an opening in the trees it looked like a nice place to sit in the shade and see what the spot had to offer him. There was a bit of a round bay just in front of where he was going to rest, it was a perfect size spot to tuck the kayak out of site. He pulled up against the coastline and first noticed that the water trickle into the rocky shore. He climbed upon the rock face and sat down on a fallen tree log he made a sandwich of stuff he packed and other things he had scavenged along the way. He was really enjoying the day with the nice breeze flowing from the lake into the tree line. After he was finished eating, he continued to sit there and just rest for a while.

After some time, he was just about ready to fall asleep then he started hearing some trickling water he was surprised he didn't hear this earlier. He stared following the noise down a trail, it took him to the top of a series of waterfalls and rapids flowing into a big round pool of water that looked to turn into a small river of its own. It was going in the same direction he needed to go so he decided it would be fun to take a scenic route on the adventure.

He went back to where he got off and climbed down to the water and started fighting to get his kayak to shore, he got it up on the land and dragged it up the rocks with him and pulled it up to the top, he packed up his belongings then set travel wheels on the kayak and wheeled it to the falls. Once he got there, he had to pick it up over his head with his belonging on his back a difficult task but for Henry it was something he had done many times in the past, he was a very experienced outdoors man. The difficult part for him in this situation was carrying it down a steep cliff, he slipped at one point and fell almost a foot and thought it was the end. Luckily, he just caught his balance on a lower rock some how he felt very agile more so then ever he figured it must be the adrenaline kicking in. Once he got to the bottom of the rock face he was at the start of the river. He put his kayak in the water just outside of the rapid's buildup he packed his belongings up nicely and started paddling his way down.

He paddled for hours through what seemed to be an endless forest. When he first got into this unknown river, he traveled past pine trees and mossy rocks. The trees he passed immediately went to beautiful hardwoods with bright majestic leaves there were clean rocks along the outside. As Henry kept paddling, he felt serenity for hours, he was alone and there was not a soul nearby. He paddled and whistled away. A while later the tree line opened ahead of him, and he got the feeling for the first time he was being watched.

Before he got to the open tree line he heard creaking through the trees, he had a very bad feeling. He looked towards where he heard the noise there was movement in the brush, and out of nowhere a branch came snapping down in the air. Then a giant beast grabbed on to him and Henry let out an awful cry. The beast was covered in fur it had the body of a man and a face of an ape; Henry knew this to be the legendary sasquatch that he never believed in. The beast let out a horrid cry, that turned Henrys cry into a ghost white pale expression on his face. The monkey man slapped Henry upside the head with contained force just enough to knock him unconscious.

When Henry awoke, he noticed there were three figures standing above him one had a great tall shape it was the big foot that he had recently met. The one in the middle was a figure that resembled a jack rabbit, but it was very great in size, and it had tall horns like an antelope. The third was also quite large, very muscular, he had rough red skin and one eye taking up most of its head. He was a very tall and strong looking Cyclops.

Henry just stared at them in shock and awe with his jaw dropped, with his heart racing, he was speechless! The horned rabbit yelled at the other two to take a step back and let Henry breath then he said, "Welcome Henry your arrival has been long overdue" Henrys face went from shock to confusion. "Don't be so startled and confused" the rabbit told him. My name is Jack the Jackalope the leader of our community." Then he pointed at the Sasquatch, and said, "Henry you have already met my friend Squatch and my other friend is known as Retina, together we protect these lands.

"What land? where the heck am I? Henry asked, in extreme confusion."

This is the Autumn River my child, we were just lucky enough for you to be traveling on a beautiful fall day to find our passage. This must mean you are the one we have been waiting for." Henry leaned his head to the side and just stared at the Jackalope. For centuries this river has existed but only a true adventurer is able to find it, that's why you're the one for the job." Henry just kept staring at him waiting for him to fill him in a little better. "There are many beings through the Autumn River, but we have been in distress for a long time. The critters of our forest dwell in these parts and used to roam all through out, that was until the pack of wolf men grew stronger. They are similar to what you know as a werewolf, but they are not human whatsoever, and they can come out in the day or whenever they choose it is their permanent form. There was a wolf that was said to been struck by a magic lightning bolt that turned out to be a curse on him. He goes by the name of Wild Tooth. He started growing the ability to stand from there he evolved and found the way to use his arms and think like us. We are the only ones here that can communicate with you and have certain gifts. The critters of these woods do not have the knowledge to speak with you, but we are the wise elders. In case you are still wondering why we need you, the beast eventually bred throughout his pack, there is now an army of them lurking and taking whatever they can.

We need you Henry because you probably know that werewolves can be penetrated by silver. We have a grand weapon that only a true adventurer has the knowledge to use. You are not the first man to come here. Before the overtaking a man left an axe with a pure silver handle and blade that he had forged himself. Retina and Squatch have both tried throwing it and it was almost lost forever it was a journey in its own getting it back. We sense that with this axe an accurate hit between the eyes would finish him and bring the rest back to their natural states. That's where you come into play that man was a master axe thrower and left us that as a gift; since you were able to find your way here you must have knowledge with axes."

Henry started thinking of all the times he had hunted with an axe and had always been quite accurate. He believed that maybe fate had brought him here, to help these strange creatures. "Well show me the axe let me see what I am working with"

"Alright now were in business!! Squatch get him up to his feet." Then the Sasquatch gave him a mighty pull to his feet. Henry thought his arm was going to come right off. He got to his feet and started dusting himself off then the Jackalope turned his back to him and said, "follow me I will show you everything you need to know about our place."

The Cyclops grabbed a rock and knocked Henry back down to the ground. When Henry woke again, he found himself in a small hole like cave, a dark space it looked to be a hole in the ground. The Jackalope stood tall in front of him almost hitting the top with his antlers, and the other two crouched on each side of him, as they were too tall to stand. "I'm sorry my child that we had to do that to you again, even though you may be the one we had foreseen we cannot have outsiders seeing our community, at least not until after you destroy our enemy. Not that I don't trust you but if you are to be captured, they have awful methods of persuading anyone to speak."

Then Jack picked up the lantern from the ceiling then lowered it down, Henry could see there was a glass case in front of him that contained a ferocious silver axe with a vicious blade and a strong curved handle. Henry gasped at it then said, wow that's the nicest blade I have ever seen."

"Do you think you can handle this vital task, if not we can send you home now."

"No sir you can count me in on this you have my total commitment"

"Well, I guess we should start our journey I warn you again it will not be fun, this time we promise not to knock you out."

"It's a deal"

Then Jack slid off the top of the glass case and said now see how it feels in your hands. Then Henry reached in and griped on to the pure silver handle. He could feel a charge of energy flow through him it looked as if it would be extremely heavy, but it felt lighter than any small hatched he had ever thrown he was able lift it just effortlessly.

"Now Mr. Henderson" The Jackalope said, "that is not the only thing you will need on our journey, here is dagger." Jack handed him a large thick bladed knife with a strong wooden handle. Jack moved the lantern towards the wall and shined it on a tall length bow with a quiver of a dozen steel arrows. "Now grab your tools Mr. Henderson and we shall be on our way to the mountain where the wolf man calls home." The Cyclops stood and put his arms up in the air and lifted a large rock from the ceiling, then the light shined into the cave. "Retina lead the way out of here." He grabbed on to the surface and pulled himself up with ease, the sasquatch did the same thing, "Now your turn Mr. Henderson. Henry walked up to the opening and reached up he could barely get a good grip to pull himself up, the two others each grabbed his arm and gave him a great yank out of the cave. Once Henry was out of the way Jack took a great leap out of the hole, he flew right over everybody and landed right in front of Henry. "Now we go!"

When they got above ground Henry seen that they were in a very thick desolate spot in the woods there was a cluster of red leafed trees all above him and around him. Jack scurried through the woods, Squatch and Retina ran behind him both had large battle axes on their back ones that would be much too heavy to throw, and they were not made of silver. Henry ran behind them doing his best to keep up, after the initial sprint they traveled at a steadier pace for hours until they could start hearing the howling of wolves. That is when Retina and Squatch pulled out their weapons; Henry could feel an uneasy sense over him, he pulled his bow off his back and made sure he was ready to shoot it at any moment. They kept moving onward until one of the beasts jumped out the tree line and leaped at Jack. Henry fired an arrow right into its skull dropping it to the ground, two more leaped out one went to attack Retina but with one slice of his axe he chopped its head clean off. Another attacked Squatch but he grabbed it by the skull and snapped its neck bringing it to the ground. The four started running again at a full pace Henry looked behind him just for a second and seen one on his tail. He shot an arrow and again it hit perfectly right between the eyes.

They finally made it out of the forest and arrived at the bottom of the mountain where the wolf men called home. They were greeted by dozens of the wild beasts Retina and Squatch went into battle mode Henry started firing arrows as quick as he could hoping not to run out.

Jack looked above and seen the leader up on a high cliff and bounced back where Henry was, he grabbed on to him and said, "let's go." Jack took one of the greatest leaps he had ever made, and they both soared up into the sky towards the cliff leaving Squatch and Retina to defend themselves. They were greatly outnumbered. Jack and Henry landed up on the cliff right in front of Wild Tooth "now you die," Jack yelled, "it's over!"

The beast looked mean and ferocious it had long dark yellow fangs with bright yellow eyes covered in mangy fur standing on its slender creepy legs. The beast immediately took a run at Henry before he could get the axe ready to throw. The Wolf Man stuck its claws right into his skin and made him bleed uncontrollably he took a bite out of his ear then he threw him over his head this sent Henry flying in the air sending him right over the edge of the cliff then Wild Tooth rushed towards Jack. The last thing Henry did as he was going over the edge was, he grabbed the silver axe and gave it everything, he had spiraling it in a wild non aimed throw that sunk right into the back of the leader's skull. Wild Tooth dropped to the ground and became nothing but a blanket of fur. The enemy's that surrounded Retina and Squatch instantly turned into regular wolves and started heading up the mountain to see their leader. Jack jumped back down to his friends, and they ran back their village.

For Henry his fate was falling from nearly a thousand feet to a shallow part of the river where he would surely be dead, but when he hit the water, he landed perfectly on his kayak and was in a whole new location. He was in a place with a big wide-open lake with pine trees all around the shoreline as he looked he realized he had made it to his destination of Big Pine lake. He sat on his canoe with all his belongs in perfect order completely confused by the situation.

He didn't know what had just happened to him, but all he knew for sure is that he just went on one a hell of a trip.

POUNDING THE KEYS

In my dimly lit room of my cramped apartment, I sat hunched over my cluttered desk, staring blankly at the blinking cursor on the darn computer screen. The soft glow of the monitor illuminated my face, highlighting the bags under my eyes and the dishevelled mop of hair on my head. I am feeling the weight of my writing inadequacy pressing down like a lead blanket.

I always fancied himself a writer—a wordsmith capable of crafting eloquent prose that would captivate readers and leave them spellbound. I dreamed of penning novels that would stand the test of time, earning me a place among the literary greats. You know, Hemingway, Angelou, and the rest. Yet in reality, I am little more than a bumbling fool with a penchant for misplaced modifiers and run-on sentences.

My fingers poised over the keyboard, but the words refused to come.

Every sentence I type felt clumsy and forced, lacking the poetic grace I so desperately sought to achieve. It felt as if a sack of potatoes had replaced my brain, with each thought clumsily tumbling over the next in a jumbled mess of nonsensical gibberish.

In a fit of frustration, I slammed my fists furiously down on the keyboard, sending a cascade of letters and punctuation marks flying across the screen in a chaotic whirlwind.

I look at the screen and there, in front of my eyes, is a short story completely written.

The story followed the journey of a curious young girl named Emily, who stumbled upon the secret world of these extraordinary cats while exploring the hidden corners of her grandmother's attic. There, amidst forgotten trinkets and dusty relics, Emily discovered an old journal filled with tales of the enigmatic felines.

'Hot darn, I hit the jackpot! I am going to be famous for this story. I can see a contract coming my way. Even a movie deal. Hollywood, here I come.' Is all I am screaming aloud.

'Is this all I need to do in the future?' I think to myself. 'Just get the keyboard in front of me and give it a good whack? Is it that simple? Has it always been this simple?' as my thoughts flood my mind.

If this is the way all the old Masters of Literature did it, no wonder it has worked for so many.

'Formidable,' I say aloud. 'That is what I call pounding the keys.'

José F Nodar © 2024.

ABOUT THE AUTHORS

Susannah Thompson

I have always been interested in human behaviour and the many ways it can be written about and interpreted. Even advertisements hold a particular interest to me. Currently I reside in the Camden area and continuing to be interested in its local history.

Curtis L. L. Herbold

When Curtis started writing, he was not the best with language skills, nor did he have a fancy car. Money was out of the question and if he emptied his pocket, dust would fall out.

Curtis never dreamt of publishing a book or becoming a "Best Selling" author.

He was just happy living his own life in a one-bedroom apartment, working in a minimum wage job, and paying his dues to society, but he did all of this without the help of his family, friends, or government.

The only help Curtis had was to get his first book edited professionally by a freelance editor.

Like all authors, he started his journey by creating the plot, the storyline, and everything else that goes into the creation of a book. Add to this the creation of his webpage, the book covers, social media platform and he was in business.

Curtis put himself out there for the world to see him and to witness his accomplishments.

Curtis once said 'Even if I do not become rich or famous off the book series, at least I get to say I did this, and I am proof of myself for accomplishing what I have, especially considering the challenges I have encountered with Asperger Syndrome. This book series it to say nothing can stop you if you put your mind to it.

Damian Nakare II

Damian Nakare II grew up in poverty in the ghetto. He was helpless, and his handicap made his childhood hard. Bullies targeted him at school and in the community. Many people tease him with funny names. But his mother encouraged him to be strong.

At age 24, he believed in the Lord Jesus. He accepted the gospel of grace. He is passionate about preaching and teaching the Bible. He also offers guidance to those going through hard times. He spreads the good news of our Lord Jesus Christ to others. He hopes to work with God, the Creator of Heaven. His book is 'The Gospel in Seven Words: clarifying John 3:16.' In this book, he offers a concise summary of the grace-based gospel.

Deena Lindstedt

Deena is a widow living in Tigard, Oregon. She has three sons, nine grandchildren, and six great-grandchildren. Following her twenty-five-year business career in workers' compensation claims administration, besides going back to college receiving her BA degree in English Literature and Writing, she devoted herself to a second marriage to Donald Lindstedt living in Cannon Beach, Oregon. Following Don's death in 2014, she moved to Tigard, Oregon to be closer to family. She is kept busy with her writing a member of P.E.O. and a bridge player.

Lady of the Play was an early 2022 award winner with Firebird Book Awards. Other fiction honors include third place winner for a poem: Two Ladies of Chedigny for Willamette Writers, Portland. Finalist for short story: Simply to Fly for NW Writers Association contest in Seattle. She presented a paper at the Virginia Woolf Conference, Lewis and Clark University and a guest speaker at the 2011 Shakespeare Authorship Symposium delivering her paper, Shakespeare, Perhaps a Woman.

She has revised her book, Deception Cove, now available as the first of the Meredith Maxwell Mystery series. She is currently writing the second book of the series, titled, Betrayal Bay.

W. D. Kilpack III

W.D. Kilpack III is an award-winning and critically acclaimed internationally published writer, with works appearing in print, online, radio and television, starting with his first publication credit at the age of nine, when he wrote an award-winning poem. As an adult, his first two novels, Crown Prince and Order of Light, both received the Firebird Book Award, while Crown Prince received The BookFest Award. He also received special recognition from L. Ron Hubbard's Writers of the Future Contest for his novella, Pale Face.

Kilpack has been editor and/or publisher of 19 news and literary publications, both online and in print, with circulations as high as 770,000.

He is an accomplished cook and has two claims he thinks few can match: cooking nearly every type of food on a grill; and nearly being knocked flat when his grill exploded.

Ellie Jay

Ellie Jay is an independent author with a love of fiction and a nasty habit of sarcasm.

She writes books of all different genres and ties them all together with sarcastic third-person narration.

At the moment, her published works include The Secrets Series, a trilogy of Russian Mafia action thrillers with dashes of sci-fi and overarching sarcasm and Planet of Lies, a sci-fi story that is packed full of witty dialogue and narration.

Jeff Webber

Jeff Webber is a former Software Engineer who grew up in Richmond, Massachusetts, he is now retired and live with his wife and mother-in-law in Western Massachusetts.

Jeff has four grown children, one son and three daughters, three of whom still lives in Massachusetts.

Jeff earned a B.S. in Mathematics from Worcester Polytechnic Institute and has done graduate work in both Applied Math and Computer Science.

He is an avid reader (mostly Science Fiction and Fantasy) since grade school.

Jeff took a long time to make his first novel (nearly 20 years) and split it into two books. Jeff spent nearly 20 years working on his first novel and then split it into two books.

The first book, Enimnori: Arrival, was finally published in December 2021, and the second book, Enimnori: Discovery, was published in September 2022.

Book three (Enimnori:Challenge) was published Aug 15,2023, with book 4 (Enimnori:Crisis) due to be released in 2024.

Grizzly G. Gus

Grizzly G. Gus is a good ole boy, and he is M. David Lutz's cousin, a famous author (or so says M. David Lutz).

Grizzly lives in a double-wide mobile home in a senior citizens' park, in Florida, now retired from the Navy and Civil Service. He spends his day (besides drinking) saying and doing things none of us would. Grizzly's works are more edgy, certainly not PG. However, Lutz pointed out an interesting point.

He stated that when Grizzly was submitting his short stories and he was doing the same to various magazines, Grizzly got published while Lutz did not.

Grizzly is happy to state that his success was such because he hired his cousin M. David Lutz to be his publisher. As his publisher, M. David Lutz is tasked with toning down Grizzly's short stories for projects, in addition to all the other requirements for publishing. Leaving Grizzly with the task of staying sober enough to write.

Grizzly has a ton of short stories. As far as social media, Grizzly has:

His own email: grizzlyggus@outlook.com

His own Facebook page: https://fb.com/grizzlyggus

However, since he is lazy, Grizzly shares M. David Lutz's website: http://www.mdavidlutz.com

One last note: My specialty is short stories, blogs, and an advice column. No matter how I beg, my cousin feels I need more of a following before he will commit to helping me publish my first book.

That is my cousin M. David Lutz.

Jenny England

Jenny worked for many years as a freelance journalist. Now retired, living in Kiama NSW Australia, she is concentrating on mastering the art of the speculative short story.

Her children's stories have been published in The School Magazine and anthologies. In 2021 she won the Nadia Lyne Writing Competition for Children's Writing.

She has earned a few awards along the way for her adult stories, which have been published in local magazines and anthologies.

When not writing, she can be found sketching or knitting for charities.

Maree Gladwin

Maree Gladwin is a Melbourne-based musician, poet, artist, and ardent traveller who loves everything queer and surprising!

With a doctorate in politics, Maree has worked in universities and the not-for-profit sector in the UK and Australia.

Her poems in English and French have been published in the Poetry D'Amour anthology, Love Poems, 2018.

Sam Prosser

Sam Prosser is a recent graduate with a degree in psychology and sociology from the University of Bath Spa in the Southwest of England. Not only does he delve into the intricacies and nuances of the human mind during the day, but he also weaves elaborate tales of his own whenever the stars align.

In the moments of free time which he manages to carve out, Sam can be found dedicated to penning his debut book, Memoirs of a Romantic—a compelling and true story of love and adventure from the perspective of his seventeen-year-old self. The story follows as Sam meets a girl on a college trip to Slovenia, and the unforgettable day they shared together before Sam returned home. Weeks of online talks and calls ensue before he finally builds up the confidence to return to Slovenia. Despite warnings from his friends and the lack of awareness from his parents, Sam sets off on his own to reunite with his holiday crush. The trip takes a few unexpected turns, however, as he finds himself stranded in Italy on Easter Sunday with no transportation and his debit card restricted. His only hope is to hitchhike the one hundred miles between him and his destination.

Seventeen and alone in a foreign country, Sam must make some difficult decisions if he is to make it to her in time. Ultimately, Memoirs of a Romantic is a tale of isolation, persistence, and the naivety that comes with love.

Sam's main interests with literature lie with the larger-than-life fantasy stories such as Harry Potter, Game of Thrones, and Mistborn, among many others. But Sam has always been a sucker for the captivating stories told in film, games, anime, and manga, and expresses a desire to one day work on projects that bring stories to life.

As Sam embarks on a career in psychology, he aspires to fulfil a lifelong ambition by leaving his own indelible mark on the world of literature. Whether it is poetry, fantasy, sci-fi, or romance, Sam is full of ideas that he dreams of putting onto paper.

M. David Lutz

M. (Mark) David Lutz is a dedicated writer, specializing in comedy and satire. He started seriously writing humor over twenty years ago. Primarily publishing articles and short stories until he turned his attention to writing a book series.

He has assisted other writers, encouraging them to develop their talents and helping them publish their projects.

Now retired after forty years of government service, Mark looks forward to writing full time.

He is regularly communicating with readers through his website and Facebook accounts while continuing to write additional volumes to his 'Princess and Plumber' series in addition to other projects.

He currently resides overseas with his wife and daughter.

Mariela Ivón Armando

Mariela Ivón Armando is a seasoned English and Spanish teacher with a master's degree in editing and editorial management from Argentina.

At 37, she not only excels in the classroom but also leads Connect Book Services, a company she founded to assist authors globally with editing, publishing, and the promotion of books. Although Mariela started writing stories at the age of 12, she stepped into the literary world as an author in February 2022 with her self-published book, "El Lado Oscuro."

Additionally, her creative prowess is showcased in several tales published by Editorial Rubin in different anthologies throughout 2023, with two more stories set to be featured in an upcoming anthology in 2024.

Mariela's multifaceted career highlights her dedication to both education and the enriching world of literature.

Mark Kramarzewski

Mark Kramarzewski was born in Sydney and now lives, works and writes in Canberra, Australia.

He is married and a father of two young children with whom he is dedicatedly instilling a love of reading, fantasy and adventure.

He enjoys building fantasy worlds for his family and friends to play and tell stories within.

M. Garnet

Muriel G. Yantiss writes un the pen name M. Garnet.

Her time owing an International Business gave her a hard view of life, but her farm family in Kentucky left her with a great humour to enjoy everything, bad and good.

Writing has allowed her to put these observations down and share with others, lacing each story with facts.

Living now in Florida with her daughter and son in law, a dog and two cats and a quaker parrot she still ends most letters with her statement: life is good.

She has many books published so look for her other titles.

Paul Backalenick

Paul Backalenick writes tales of psychological suspense and moral conflict. His first novel, Development, is a thriller set within a family drama. His second book, Carrie's Secret, is a mystery that takes place in a mental hospital. His third novel is Empty Luck, a fast-paced thriller of crime and passion in Las Vegas.

In all his writing, Paul is interested in questions of ethical behavior. Morality, or the lack of it, underpins all his stories.

Paul studied creative writing at Brown University with a concentration in psychology. He is a supporter of animal rights, ecology and conservation causes. He enjoys playing piano, poker, and golf, and traveling as much as possible. Born in Boston, he grew up in Westport, Connecticut and now lives in New York City with his wife, artist Karen Loew.

Peter Draper

Peter Draper was born in Northfleet, Kent in the UK and grew up in the area. Following a very brief stint in the military, he had a variety of jobs that eventually took him to America and Canada.

In 1995, he took up skydiving and very quickly became an instructor and certificated parachute rigger, a skill that he took to a major parachute equipment manufacturing company. He eventually racked up over 7,000 jumps, many as a tandem instructor taking people on their first ever skydives,

This, in turn, led to working with the Qatar Armed Forces, where, for over 10 years, he worked for the Qatar Joint Special Forces (Airborne) until his retirement in 2020. During his time in Qatar, he trained with many elite groups from around the world, including the Italian Folgare and the French Foreign Legion amongst others.

He now lives in The Philippines with his wife Veronica.

Sai Marie Johnson

Sai Marie Johnson is an Oregon novelist, independent journalist, and freelance designer with over a decade's worth of experience.

She has worked with NYT, USA Today, and Amazon's best-selling authors in addition to providing consulting on author services, public relations, marketing, and branding.

A passionate activist and author Sai Marie Johnson has dedicated her life to the advocacy of of important issues such as social justice, racism, sexism, human trafficking and genetic research for Duchenne's Muscular dystrophy.

She has a reputation for asking the tough questions and holding people accountable at the highest levels.

Thomas Greenbank

Thomas Greenbank writes gritty Australian fiction. His debut novel, GOLD! The Kincaid Saga Book 1 was a finalist in the respected 2020 Page Turner Awards.

Greenbank's writing draws deeply on his diverse background and professional experience.

From years as a professional musician, factory worker, business owner, driver, ceramic artist, crossword compiler, copywriter and more—including 25 years as a full-time carer—there's not much he hasn't experienced. This diversity shows in his writing, as does his penchant for accuracy in research.

Now semi-retired, Thomas lives south of Adelaide, South Australia, with his wife — #1 fan and chief collaborator — Linda. When he's not writing, you'll probably find them fishing or walking on a nearby beach.

Peter McCollum

An expatriate of 10+ years, Peter resides in Thailand.

He is known to frequent outdoor markets, medical dispensaries, and every new 7-11 that pops up in his district.

Dr Robin Craig

Dr Robin Craig is a scientist and philosopher who enjoys writing dramatic and engaging stories driven by strong characters and intriguing philosophical themes: stories you love to read that make you think.

His main subjects are near future science fiction exploring contemporary issues like artificial intelligence and human genetic engineering, but other themes include time travel, historical fiction, fantasy and short stories.

Doug Jacquier

Doug Jacquier is the editor of the humour site, Witcraft.

Based on the Fleurieu Peninsula in South Australia, his own work has been published in Australia, the US, the UK, Canada, New Zealand, and India.

Jesse Calnan

Jesse Calnan is a budding author with a passion for weaving captivating tales.

"Way of the Ghosts," his debut collection of short stories, explores the mysterious and the richness of the people he writes about.

He spends his free time devouring as many books as possible to enrich his own writing.

He is currently working on fantasy series, that focuses on a magic land with many original characters and creatures. He has had the idea for a decade and fooled around with different thoughts.

Now he is committed to working on it and hopes to have the first book released some point this year of 2024.

José F. Nodar

The Cuban revolution in 1959 presented José with one of his many life challenges. José was born in La Habana; Cuba and the Cuban revolution saw him get on a plane alone at eleven years of age and arrive at an orphanage in the small town of Washington, Georgia. He did not get to see his parents again until he was eighteen years old and had graduated from high school in Atlanta, Georgia.

He studied Business Administration at Georgia State University. From university, he headed into the finance world working for the First National Bank of Atlanta (now Wells Fargo) and then moved into the financial consulting world working as a project manager, travelling to many assignments in the United States, Europe, and Australia.

José began writing his debut novel after getting his feet wet in creative writing at a writers' group in Camden New South Wales, Australia. This gave him 'the bug' as he calls it and soon his mind created his first major character, Danny Monk.

Currently, José is working on his sixth collection of short stories and a sequel to his novel *'Books, Pens, and Larceny'* due out later in the year or early 2025.

When José is not writing you can find him sitting at the local shopping centre mall watching people and getting inspiration for his future characters.

When not in front of his computer working away, José is reading or spending time with his wife in long, leisurely walks around the Camden area.

www.ingramcontent.com/pod-product-compliance
Lightning Source LLC
Chambersburg PA
CBHW061100100726
47911CB00012B/322